THE WENDIGO HUNTER

A GOTHIC HORROR NOVELLA

KATHLEEN GREER

Crystal Cove Press
*A Young Adult Speculative Fiction Imprint
of Crystal Lake Publishing*

crystalcovepress.com

CHAPTER ONE

"Say, Jo. What is that child doing?"

Rob leaned forward, pointing with the carriage reins at a swarthy-skinned boy near the bend in the road ahead. The boy appeared to be digging in a mound of leaves; the scent of mildew, perhaps mould permeated the breeze.

The child rose, much taller than expected, his dark eyes wide. Oily black hair fell across his forehead. He looked frightened, like so many of the gypsies who worked the New Hampshire farms in the summer and fall. They were known for their thievery and lies.

Hanging from the boy's left hand was a long brown log. At his feet lay a bouquet of bright yellow lilies, dappled in the afternoon sunlight cascading through the tree limbs overhead.

"Hey, you there. What are you about?" Rob's words sounded angry.

The boy dropped the log onto the ground and took off at a furious pace, the bottoms of his bare feet slipping on the damp leaves. But not before grabbing the bouquet of flowers as he ran away. Within seconds, he disappeared into the dark oak forest that surrounded this side of the lake. A forlorn shovel remained behind, lying in the grass.

"Well, that was damned strange," Rob muttered, climbing down from the carriage.

Up ahead, a huge man, at least eight feet tall if not more, stood by the side of the road leading into Melvin Village. Stark naked, he held a bow curled in his right fist. A finely tooled leather bag of arrows swung from his back. A long braid of dark brown hair curled over his shoulder. When he turned to look at me, his eyes glowed amber, as though the fires of hell burned in his belly.

I blinked, then blinked again.

Suddenly, the acrid odor of smelling salts invaded my senses.

I woke to Rob and Isobel wafting the air in front of my face.

"Jo, are you all right?" Rob held my right hand so tightly my fingers ached. Was that a tear rolling down his left cheek? I hadn't meant to cause such a scene.

"She's fine, Rob. Just a little fall." My sister slipped a bottle of smelling salts into her skirt pocket.

Then she grinned at me.

"Sister, I've talked with you about such unseemly behavior." Isobel was clearly enjoying her role.

Rob's strong arm lifted me into a sitting position, and I realized I had tumbled out of the carriage.

"This is quite embarrassing," I murmured, wondering what else to say. Maybe Rob could explain what had happened. I met his eyes and sensed the glimmer of a smile. "I saw the most frightening apparition," I continued. His expression darkened as he brushed back a lock of his dark brown hair.

"What sort of apparition?" he asked, leaning me into the crook of his muscular leg, his right arm behind my shoulder.

"A giant of a man. An Indian, standing right there, where the boy was digging. His eyes glowed with the fires of Hell."

Isobel began to giggle behind us. "A giant Indian. Really, Jo."

Rob completely ignored her. "Go on," he said quietly.

"That's it. He was just standing there, completely naked. Just a bow and a sack of silver-tipped arrows on his back. He turned and looked at me over his shoulder, and his eyes—they glowered like hot embers or coals. Then you woke me up. What do you think happened to me?"

"I'm not sure, but let's see if we can find out."

Rob gently lifted me to my feet, and we all walked to where the gypsy boy had been digging in the leaves. Rob's face paled as he reached the hole, and he held up his hand in warning.

"Isobel shouldn't see this. It appears to be some sort of grave."

"Are you serious?" I said, then stopped as I reached the hole and looked inside.

I quickly backed away. "Good Lord, what was that boy burying?" The stench of mold was overpowering.

"More like, what was he digging up?" said Isobel, who had somehow snuck up behind us.

She bent over as though to pick up something, but Rob grabbed her arm. "Don't touch anything," he said quietly, and from his stance, it was obvious he was quite perturbed.

"We know nothing about this body other than it has been in a state of decay for a long time. We don't know what the body died from; the bones could be diseased."

Isobel drew back, holding her hand out in front of her as though it were contaminated, but with what?

"Is it the Indian I saw?" They both turned toward me then, as though they'd forgotten my existence.

Rob spoke, and for the first time, a certain firmness tinged his words. This was the man I knew and loved. The past few months he'd seemed distant, bored, but not today.

"You saw a giant of a man," he repeated. "If so, then yes, it could be, for these bones are those of a huge individual. Verily, a giant of a man. But why he was buried here is beyond me. The Melvin Village church is some half mile from here, and the graveyard is up on the knoll overlooking the lake."

I found myself whispering, my eyes drawn to the edge of the grave. "If he was an Indian, perhaps they couldn't bury him in hallowed ground."

Though the sun was bright, I shivered. In truth, why had the gypsy boy been digging this grave up? And the day lilies he'd run away with? Had he meant to place them on the grave?

Isobel drew closer to the gravesite. Face pale, she looked down into the open pit and cried out softly. "Why was he left here like this?" One hand trembled at her lips. "Buried with no headstone, like a pauper, yet worse, for he was buried naked as the day he was born. It is too sad for words."

"I don't suppose there's a constable to be had in these parts?" I asked.

Rob's expression spoke volumes.

"No, of course not," I interrupted, before he had a chance to speak. "So we can try and cover him back up. The boy did leave that shovel behind."

"Oh, surely not," Isobel cried out.

For a moment, she appeared to sway, and I grabbed her arm, afraid she would tumble into the grave.

"Isobel, animals will tear apart what is left of him, carry the bones to the far ends of the earth. We can't leave him like this," I added gently. My sister had always been too sensitive.

Isobel sank to the ground, and Rob seized her hands and knelt by the grave beside her.

"Isobel, don't cry. There aren't that many bones left of him."

Isobel really began to cry in response. If this was Rob's attempt at humour, he needed to work on his delivery.

"God spare me from my sister's tears," I muttered, but I did glance into the grave at that point and instantly realized Rob was right. Only a few gigantic bones rested in the dark loamy soil; no head, no torso. Just two tibias, a humerus, and one enormous femur.

Plus, a rotted leather sack full of silver-tipped arrows, which appeared to be in remarkably good condition. Just like the ones carried by the apparition I'd seen standing in the road. Yet there was no way I had known anyone was buried at this spot...or who.

Indeed, this was the first time we'd taken this route. Normally we stayed in Wolfeboro and headed to the White Mountains on the carriage road leading from there.

A soft breeze stirred the mouldy leaves at my feet. The hairs on the back of my neck prickled beneath my soft cotton collar. Dappled sunlight flitted across the unmarked grave by the lake. For the briefest of seconds, I fancied the giant thigh bone moved against the black earth.

"We need to get out of here," I whispered and grabbed Isobel's shoulder, pulling her backward, away from the grave.

Coming to his feet, Rob stared at me in disbelief. "We can't leave the grave like this," he said. "You just agreed we need to cover it back up."

"Yes, we can leave, and we will. Arthur Cavendish can decide what is best. He has servants to handle emergencies like this. Miramar Hall isn't that far away. This might even be on his land for all we know. Let's go, now. Come, Isobel."

My sister scrambled into the carriage behind me, lips pressed tight, cheeks so pale her skin appeared translucent.

"I think sister is right, Rob," she cried out. "Something is wrong here. Something we shouldn't get involved with. I wish we'd never seen that gypsy boy." She shrank against the inside wall of our carriage, huddled under the dark carriage robe.

Despite the warmth of the afternoon sun, I shivered and drew a shawl around my own shoulders.

"Let's not speak of it again," I whispered.

Somehow, though, I knew the apparition I'd seen was not gone for good.

CHAPTER TWO

"Good Lord, you two are quite the pair, aren't you? As if my son's care isn't enough to occupy your time, you had to bring dead giants into the mix."

Arthur Cavendish appeared mildly irritated, hand on one stout hip as he swirled a glass of amber whiskey before taking a deep swig. A large emerald gleamed from his left pinkie, while the twinkle in his green eyes told a different story.

Rob took a deep drink from his own glass of malt. He winked at Josie before continuing his recitation of the day's events. Isobel was seated in the corner with Jason Cavendish, drinking a small glass of raffia wine while they played Rummy after dinner.

"Well, my thanks for sending your men to see to the problem," said Rob.

"Ah, damned gypsies. They are all over the countryside this time of year. You can't trust a single one of those lying thieves. The farmers need their help bringing in the early summer crops, especially the hay, so the fields will produce a second crop before winter."

For a brief moment, Jo was back on the farm, tossing hay with Sly and the others, as strong as any of the men. The sun felt warm on her back, sweat trickling down between her breasts. *Heave, Ho.*

Heave, Ho. Much like a ship, they all moved in unison to the sound of the beater.

"Jo, Mr. Cavendish asked you a question."

She glanced up at the two men from where she sat on an embroidered settee. Rob winked again. "My wife was daydreaming, no doubt. She grew up on a farm, Arthur, so is well aware of what you speak. Right, darling?"

Jo fought down the desire to snort. Rob would pay for his comments later tonight.

"Yes, such fond memories of the farm," she said, coming to her feet. "What did you want to know, Mr. Cavendish?"

"Arthur, please," the stout man said. "I was just telling your husband about the ancient tales concerning the Indians, the so-called Red Men who once inhabited these lands. They had no written word, so the stories were carried by mouth from generation to generation, down through thousands of years. I was asking if you'd ever heard any of their tales?"

Jo looked at him quizzically. "Thousands of years? Really, Mr. Cavendish. Surely you exaggerate?"

"I am more than serious, young woman. Long before the Mohawks, Iroquois, and Algonquins hunted these forests, aboriginal Indians fished the rivers and shores. Even the Bible speaks of giants who roamed the woods. And what of the tale of Chocorua? No one has ever found his grave, though he supposedly jumped from a huge rock at the top of a mountain. Is that another exaggeration?"

What a strange man. Though he carried extra weight around his middle, his cheeks were sunken, as though he'd been ill for a while.

Jo glanced over to where Jason and Isobel no longer shuffled cards but sat spellbound, listening to Arthur Cavendish's words.

"I've heard of the Algonquins, but giants? No," Rob interjected, coming to her side. He placed his hand on her shoulder. "And the Bible was written on another continent. How could it be speaking of giants here?"

"So now you question the Bible?" Arthur asked. "After some of the things we saw together during the great rebellion, surely you haven't gone atheist on me."

Across the room, Jason began to cough as he rose to his feet, his cheeks bright red. "You knew my father during the war?" he choked out. "I knew there had to be a reason my father recommended you as a doctor... So no doubt you would share my secrets with him."

A woman clad in black strode into the library, her features set, her brow furrowed.

"Alison, you've decided to join us," Jason muttered, clearly displeased. "Why weren't you at dinner?"

The attractive woman ignored his words and walked to one of the many built-in mahogany cupboards lining the room, pulling out a tattered leather volume.

"A curse upon ye, white men!" she pronounced. "May the Great Spirit curse ye when he speaks in the clouds, and his words are fire!"

"This is the story my father should have told you," the woman continued. "Chocorua had a son—and ye killed him while the sky looked bright! Lightning blast your crops! Wind and fire destroy your dwellings! The Evil Spirit breathe death upon your cattle!"

The woman looked up from the book and smiled at them all, but there was no warmth on her thin lips.

"Your graves lie in the warpath of the Indian! Panthers howl and wolves fatten over your bones! Chocorua goes to the Great Spirit—his curse stays with the white men!"

Complete silence fell, broken only by the snap and crackle of the logs burning in the enormous fireplace at the back of the room.

"I like this other poem better, though," the woman suddenly said, stepping atop the embroidered settee Jo had vacated. An already tall woman, at least six inches more than Jo, her shadow cast eerie flickers around the room, backdropped by the roaring fireplace. Her voice rang true, lending an almost sing-song quality to the words of poetry she read.

> *"And thus the story oft is told,*
> *Of all the forgotten souls...*
> *Chocorua hateful here of old,*
> *Brought maledictions many.*
> *"Curse on yer white man's soul," he prayed.*
> *Curse on yer living and the dead."*

Hand to heart, Alison continued, much louder now.

> *"Vile, heartless knaves. Ye killed my boy,*
> *My own Keoka's darling joy,*
> *Ere in the grave she rested;*
> *By deadly drugs laid low he died,*

Me too ye 've slain! let devils deride
Ye, tortured, damned, detested.

"Ho! let the war-whoop lead the fight.
The torch, the tomahawk at night,
Yer habitations storming;
Drive deep the axe, the scalping blade,
Spare never a white man, child, or maid;
Give carnage to the morning.

"Great Spirit let thy lightnings flash,
Thy fiery vengeance let it dash,
Down where the paleface prowls,
On Campbell's head, on all he owns,
Let panthers perch upon his bones,
While hot in hell he howls."

Thus prayed Chocorua, bleeding, slain;
Vengeance from thence eternal came.
Destruction dreadful, certain.
Strange now in shadows stands the sun;
The Indian hunter's day is done,
In these New England borders.

Alison's voice drifted off to a whisper.

> *Great God, forgive our Saxon race,*
> *Blot from thy book no more to trace,*
> *The sky above and earth beneath.*
> *With dearth and death eternal."*

Someone began to clap, low and slow, as Jason's dark-haired sister took her father's hand and stepped down from the settee. She glanced around the room, for the first time paying attention to her father's guests.

Rob began to laugh as she approached, and Jo felt the first tinges of jealousy tear at her heart. This woman was not only tall but limber, with flowing hair let loose about her square shoulders. She was dressed much like a man might be, in dark trousers and a black silk shirt. But there was no man beneath that clothing, only firm breasts and long legs. The woman represented everything Jo had no chance of ever becoming. Alison had been born a lady, no matter what she wore.

"I'm very pleased your last name is Cavendish, not Campbell," said Rob, making light of the dire poem she'd just read aloud. "Old Chocorua's curse sounds downright evil."

"Perhaps his fate was just as evil," said Alison, accepting a glass of red wine from her father. "But why are you all speaking of Indian curses?" she asked, taking a sip.

"While traveling here, they saw a gypsy boy digging in the woods," replied her father. "When confronted, he ran away."

"Alison tossed her dark hair over her shoulder. "Of course he did, father. They always run away. Was he digging up someone's grave?"

"A giant's grave," Isobel whispered, coming to Jo's side.

"Oh pooh, child. A giant. There are no giants, except perhaps in business. Right, Jason?"

Her brother appeared unable to speak, once again coughing repeatedly. While Jo suspected his sister was the cause of Jason's distress, apparently Rob thought otherwise. "Come, Jason. Have a sip of whiskey. These stories have given us all quite a shock."

"Leave me be," Jason gasped out, pushing past them all. "You have no idea what you're talking about," he muttered, leaving the library door open as he rushed away.

Jo seized the opportunity. "Let's go to bed, Isobel. It's been a long day and we're all tired. Are you coming, Rob?" She threw him what she hoped appeared to be an arch look, then realized it fell upon his back.

"I'll be up in a while," he said, pouring more red wine into Alison's glass. "It's been years since Arthur and I have had some time to talk."

But instinctively, Jo knew her husband's interest was in the daughter, not the father.

***

The storm that night was so strong, so terrible, Jo found it easy to spend the night huddled with Isobel. By eleven o'clock, when Rob hadn't returned to their room and the thunder overhead became so fierce she found screaming useless, she ran down the hallway and slipped into Isobel's room, where she discovered her sister cowering under the covers.

Their life on the farm had prepared them for storms like this—torrential sheets of rain and dangerous winds which could lift a building clear off its foundation.

The lightning that night, however, surrounded Miramar Hall with white-hot bolts piercing the earth, casting the immense structure onto some surreal plain where night and day mixed as fire arrows shot into the ground. One glance out the mullioned window panes sent Jo sneaking back into the bed with her sister, and together they repeated the Lord's Prayer until they both fell asleep out of sheer exhaustion.

Rob looked in on them hours later, having retired to his suite only to discover his wife missing. He quietly closed Isobel's door, relieved Jo was exactly where he suspected she might be.

They would need to talk in the morning.

He was at fault, and he needed to apologize for leaving her alone.

Hopefully, she wouldn't be too angry to listen. However, something strange was going on in this house, and he couldn't quite put his finger on it.

He'd heard the hint in his wife's voice earlier, but the lure of speaking with Arthur and observing Alison for more telltale traits held far too much allure. He hadn't realized his Boston practice had become so boring until that morning when they saw the gypsy urchin at the giant Indian's grave. All the excitement—along with some fear—of their first trip five years earlier, when he'd first met Josie, came flooding back.

Try as much as he could to deny being drawn to the occult, to the dark underworld that surrounded much of everyday life, he could not deny the tingling sensation he'd felt that morning when he looked down into the dank miasma of that long-forgotten grave and realized there was an immense mystery waiting to be solved.

That Jason's sister portrayed some of the same nervous traits as her brother just added another layer to the game. The gnawing of her bottom lip; the way she unconsciously twisted her hair around her fingers and pulled on it as though she wished to rip it from her head. Something was wrong with both of Arthur's children, and Rob had no idea what the source of so much agitation could be.

Moreover, something about Arthur seemed off as well. Much time had passed since they'd last talked, but there seemed to be no explanation for how the man had accumulated so much wealth in the past few years. The funds at his disposal seemed endless.

Twenty years his elder, Arthur had been his captain during the war between the states. At that time, Arthur held large holdings of timber and land in New Hampshire. When they met up again some ten years later, Arthur had expanded into shipping, which made sense due to the natural resources, especially forests at his disposal.

Yet somehow, in those past ten years, the man's interests had become a vast empire reaching across the ocean to England and beyond. Arthur had become a true shipping tycoon.

Still, it was the man's railroad interests that surprised Rob. His own brother Jericho had instilled in Rob a profound interest in American railroads, and he'd invested in several over the past twenty years. While some had failed, the majority had not, and he'd made a substantial amount of money himself from those invest-ments.

But while Rob was not a poor man, the riches Arthur spoke about seemed almost obscene. The man didn't invest in railroads; he built them from the ground up.

So many questions jumbled in his mind, it was just as well Jo slept in another room tonight. Rob doubted he'd find much sleep himself.

He poured several fingers of whiskey and settled into a stuffed leather armchair large enough to hold a bear. While Alison and Jason were both enigmas, the biggest question twisting his mind into knots dealt with his own practice, his own life.

When had he become so bored with his patients that he'd stopped paying attention to his own wife? He loved Jo beyond dis-traction, but somehow he had stopped listening to her concerns, her desires. If you'd asked him what they'd had for dinner the night before, he couldn't answer. Nor did he recall what they'd talked about.

Ultimately, he had to admit he couldn't remember what half his patients had complained about a week ago. So many of their stories were so similar he could interchange his replies from patient to patient.

He'd tried to give his wife and her sister a normal life. No ho-cus-pocus; no more ghosts and spirits. Just work and school.

Normal. Or so he told himself.

The problem was, he had enough money, not to mention his wife's, so there was no actual need for him to work. Indeed, he'd never taken Jo on a real vacation, or a trip to Europe, to France or Scotland or far-away Greece where they could dine on olives, cucumbers, and yogurt. Instead, for a honeymoon, they'd gone to the New Hampshire coast for a weekend and eaten lobster.

What sort of husband was he, actually? Pretending he was too busy to vacation when he hadn't received any joy from his practice in a long time.

The reality was, he had no idea what to do with himself.

For years before meeting Jo, he'd hunted down medical fakes and fraudsters, exposing them to the public. The tarot readers and Ouija board practitioners who claimed to decipher illnesses from the spirits, when they simply practiced one of the oldest arts: deception. Over the span of almost twenty years, he'd come to realize the occult world existed in the most unlikely of places; in a necklace heralding from ancient lands, in a moonlit pond, in a watch created for a dead French queen.

Yet he had ignored it all for the past five years.

From the day he asked Jo to marry him, he had disavowed any connection to the occult—or to his own abilities.

To the very truth of his existence.

Rob sighed and drained his whiskey, putting the cut crystal glass on the table beside him. Despite how much he wished to ignore the truth, the real charlatan was himself. By refusing to accept the unthinkable, he had not only put himself in danger, but possibly Jo and Isobel as well.

And clearly, his wife wasn't happy.

His wife. The words had such an odd ring to them. As if Josie would ever belong to anyone other than herself.

He walked to the farthest closet at the back of the bedroom, where, behind his great coat, rested Boromar. The ivory cane literally leaped into his hand when he called to it.

Stroking the ebony wolf's head handle, Rob sighed again as calmness entered his mind. The time had come for a change.

He would no longer deny himself the very thing he urged his patients to experience the most.

Life.

CHAPTER THREE

Alison Cavendish drew several large circles on the canvas before her. She leaned back and perused her work, then threw down her brush in disgust.

"This is going nowhere, Rob. I have about as much artistic ability as that crow over there."

Across from them, Jason feverishly dabbed at his own canvas. First here, then there. Since their canvases faced each other, she had no idea what he was working on.

One of Dr. Radnor's therapies, no doubt. The previous night she had agreed to help the doctor work with her brother, mostly out of curiosity. She had learned long ago to keep her enemies close—but she had also discovered she desired no friends. Not that Dr. Radnor, Rob as he insisted she call him, was considered an enemy.

Quite the opposite, in fact. A fascinating man and handsome beyond belief, with that chocolate brown hair just beginning to gray at the temples. Why did he have to be married?

All the interesting ones were always married. Not that it had deterred her in the past. Success often just took more maneuvering.

"What do you see when you look at those circles?" Rob asked, coming to her side. Unlike most of the men she knew, he didn't smell of cigars and horses, but of some light cologne, almost feminine in odor. Yet it suited him well, and if the circumstances were different, she would have tempted him with a kiss.

"Oh, I don't know, doctor. Perhaps watermelons in a field in fall, fat and ready to be eaten." Her laugh sounded a little too gay, and she pouted to offset the effect. Mustn't overdo things too early. "What do you see?"

"I see three shimmering ponds in the spring, just as the ice melts. The water is crystal clear, transparent to great depths where water nymphs dance."

Alison drew back in surprise. She hadn't expected such a poetic reply.

"What a coincidence," Jason interrupted. "I've drawn what else lurks in those ponds. You wouldn't catch me going in that water."

Alison sighed. The world always revolved around her brother; she couldn't wait until he was out of the picture.

Rob went to her brother's side, and his brown eyes crinkled in what she assumed was distaste. "Where did you get that image from?" he asked, peering closely at the canvas.

Alison came to her brother's other side and stared at the picture he had painted. Jason had always been artistically inclined, but this picture was more hideous than anything she could imagine.

"Good God, Jason. What gruesome things lurk in *your* mind?"

"God has nothing to do with it," he replied. "This came to me as we stood out here in the sunlight, and I recalled the poem you read last night about Chocorua."

"That is no Indian," she said flatly, drawing away. Jason's painting was downright disturbing. In a peaceful green valley ensconced by immense mountains, a crystal blue lake rested in the sunlight, surrounded by tall grasses and lilies. There, on the surface, floated a lone white swan. Below the surface, beneath its feet, sank the limbs of a dismembered body—no head, no torso. Just legs and arms, while at the ends of the disarticulated joints, small fish pulled at pieces of flesh.

"They look like schools of piranhas," Rob said, staring intently at the painting. "Is that what you dreamed about last night, Jason? After playing cards with Isobel and listening to her chatter about the body we found?"

Jason flushed darkly. "I certainly didn't dream of your ward," he replied stiffly.

Rob laughed aloud at the younger man's response and clapped him on the back. "I was just kidding. Actually, I find your artwork rather fascinating, despite your sister's revulsion."

Much like a cat, Alison veritably hissed at them. "You have to be kidding. That isn't talent; that isn't even artwork." She turned on her heel and quickly headed back in the direction of Miramar Hall, clearly disgusted.

A wide grin worked its way across Jason's ruddy face, and both men burst into laughter. Having the morning to themselves couldn't be a bad thing. Rob watched Alison's long strides, the stiffness of her back as she almost ran toward the immense stone house at the top of the ridge. Strangely, he felt sorry for her. Clearly, she wanted men to perceive her as a woman of the world—experienced and in control of any situation.

Much like her brother had described her back in Boston.

The only problem: the image didn't match reality.

Isolated behind those stone walls, she had grown up spoiled, opinionated, but without experience... and perhaps a trifle scared. Of exactly what, he wasn't sure. Maybe just the world in general.

Still, there was plenty of time ahead to help both of Arthur's children come to grips with their fears.

"Cap'n, I'm telling you, the gold is missing!"

"Wiley, lower your voice and stop calling me that! I've told you to be careful."

"Sorry, cap'n. I mean, sir."

Arthur Cavendish strode into the carriage house at the far back of Miramar Hall, bending to walk beneath the two-hundred-year-old oak beams that framed the entryway. Behind him, three wizened men hauled an iron chest between them, straining to lift it through the doorway.

"This is all we found," said Wiley, the youngest of the three, though he looked near to death as they lowered the trunk to the floor.

White oak pillars rose overhead, a testimony to the immense size of the rafters hewn from the canopy that once surrounded the lush lawns of Miramar Hall. Constructed two centuries earlier on the shores of Lake Winnipesaukee, Miramar was riddled with mystery, not the least of which included the iron chest resting in the middle of the floor.

"Like I told you, this is all we could find," said Wiley, wiping sweat from the end of his long nose. "That and them bones we left behind. Brought you the thigh bone like you asked. Smells something awful it does. We left it in the wagon."

His southern drawl sounded out of place in the New Hampshire countryside, but then everything about the three men had nothing to do with the North.

"Well, put the bone in the storage shed out behind the old privies. No one will notice the odor, not that anyone goes out there any longer." Arthur drew a long iron key from his pants pocket and inserted it into the trunk. "Let's see what you found."

It took a few minutes to get the old lock to turn. Not surprising, since the chest had been buried in the Indian's grave for over ten years. Arthur took his time, afraid the key might bend or break if forced. Finally, with a loud click, the hasp released, and he lifted the dome lid.

Wiley whistled low. His right eye, damaged during the war, lolled to the right. "Well, looky there, cap'n. We got ourselves some more gold." He picked up one of the coins, turning it over and over like he hadn't seen one before.

"You men will all get paid in gold tonight, like always." Arthur took the coin from Wiley's fingertips. "But not before you get that thigh bone into the shed. I don't want one of the servants smelling it and making a fuss."

After they had gone, Arthur went to the far back wall of the carriage house and twisted one of the round newel post tops that graced the ancient staircase leading to the attic above. In the middle of the back wall, a cavernous black hole slowly appeared as part of the wooden wall slid behind itself.

Arthur's forebearers had secrets of their own, not the least of which was their allegiance to England during the Revolutionary War. It was this allegiance that had enabled his family to make connections overseas that stood them well later during the Civil War as well. He might have fought for the North, but he had secretly sided with the South, often acting as a spy. If not for his friendship with George Trenholm, treasurer of the Confederacy, his own family's future would not be so financially secure.

Making sure his workers hadn't returned, Arthur opened an enormous safe inside the secret room and took out three pigskin bags of gold. No reason his men needed to know they were being shortchanged. Poor Crackers all, not a one of them could count past ten. They would be pleased with their share.

Grunting loudly, he slowly pushed the dome-topped iron trunk across the polished oak floor and into the hidden room.

You could never be too careful, he'd learned long ago. Now he just needed to teach Jason the same lesson.

CHAPTER FOUR

Brightly colored banners blew in the stiff breeze off Lake Winnipesaukee as Arthur Cavendish's carriage entered the town of Wolfeboro. The annual Fourth of July summer festival was already in full swing. Food vendors hawked fried dough and iced tea, while a fundraising chicken barbecue, complete with buttered corn, raised money for hundreds of war veterans who ate for free. Out on the big lake, skiffs chased along the waves in a race for dominance, while youngsters ran across the newly mowed town commons, lips smudged with traces of chocolate cookies.

Isobel's blonde curls bounced like sausages as she strained to take it all in from their carriage seat. "Oh, this will be such fun. Look, Sister. There are gypsies here too." They drove by an encampment of tattered wagons towards the back of the commons, and finally found a spot large enough for Arthur's carriage. While the older man and his daughter had begged off, saying their allergies always flared in the outdoors, Jason had been excited to attend, which made for a perfect foursome.

Jo watched Isobel grab Jason's hand. The two made a handsome couple, and observing them, she wasn't quite sure how she felt about that.

"Rob, make sure Isobel doesn't pester Jason all day," she found herself saying as she pulled her straw hat into place and drew the ribbons tight under her chin. The sun, the bane of every redhead, would leave her cheeks with a new trickle of freckles by nightfall.

"He doesn't look very pestered to me." Rob grinned as Isobel pulled Jason along, headed to the barbecue tents. "If anything, we might want to make sure they don't slip off into the woods. I think Isobel is a little too young for motherhood."

Jo slapped his shoulder with her ivory-handled fan. "Keep your voice down. Isobel would never engage in such behavior. Have you forgotten how she lectures me constantly on decorum?"

"That's because she always gets a rise out of you. I think Isobel is quite capable of most anything."

Jo's lips pursed, but she couldn't contain the giggle that slipped out. Rob was still the most infuriating...and the most handsome... She ran her fingertips over his slightly graying sideburns, then pulled his face down for a kiss. She didn't care who saw them. They were married, weren't they?

"I wonder where your mind is wandering," she whispered before brushing her lips against his.

"The same place it always wanders," he whispered back, pulling her close. "Under your skirts."

She giggled again but slipped out of his grasp. People were beginning to stare. There was no need to embarrass Isobel even more.

The afternoon flew by, complete with a band and many former Union soldiers who gamely marched in time, some missing a foot or leg, others with crutches or wooden stumps. It was sad to see how many had been wounded, but these men were heroes, proud to celebrate their heritage.

Rob had fallen asleep on the red checkered blanket they'd spread on the lawn, and Jo's head rested in his lap, the sun beginning to slip down behind the majestic oaks dotting the commons.

She was just slipping off herself when Isobel whispered in her ear, "Sister, come with me. You need to hear what the gypsy woman has to say."

Jo quietly pushed up and got to her feet. Rob continued to snore. Putting her finger to her lips, Jo walked a few feet away. "Where is Jason?" she asked quietly, reluctant to wake Rob unless it was urgent.

"He stayed behind with the gypsies," Isobel said. "Seriously, Jo. You need to talk with them." She began to pull at Jo's hand. "Come along. Rob doesn't need to know."

Jo sighed. Every time Isobel said "Rob doesn't need to know," it always turned out he did need to know. Still, until she found out what sort of trouble Isobel had gotten into this time, she would let him sleep.

"Why in the world would you two go to the gypsy camp?" she asked, walking towards the encampment. Barefoot boys hunched over dice games, chewing on straw.

"Jason wanted to see if any of them knew about the Indian grave."

Jo seriously doubted this was Jason's idea but kept quiet.

"See, they have a fortune-telling tent over there." Isobel pulled her towards a scarlet-topped tent. A flag with an all-seeing eye painted white in the middle danced from a pole at the side of the tent.

On a wooden bench outside sat Jason Cavendish, head bowed. As they neared, he looked up, his features pinched, his skin the color of parchment.

"Oh, Jason. What has happened?" Isobel kneeled at his side, her blue petticoats billowing in the wind. "You went in alone, didn't you? Why didn't you wait for me? What did she tell you?"

A wizened, dark-skinned old woman stuck her head out of the tent, casting a stern glance in their direction. Jo realized the woman only had one eye, and a cloudy one at that. How could she possibly "see" the future or the past?

"You, the older one. Come with me now," the crone said, her voice surprisingly deep and forceful.

Isobel came to Jo's side. "Not without me, she doesn't." She slid her arm around Jo's waist and gave it a squeeze.

"Little one, are you sure you want to know?" the old crone said.

"We are sisters. Of course, I want to know."

"Then come inside, but don't complain later about the truth."

The woman was so odd, Jo felt a niggling doubt creep up her spine. She should have woken Rob.

Inside the tent, a faint haze of smoke drifted in the air. A large crystal ball sat atop a rosewood stand in the middle of a round table covered by a black silk cloth. The gypsy woman wiped her palms on her dark green gingham skirt, then placed them on either side of the crystal ball, which immediately began to glow. Her eyelids closed as she began to chant.

"Oh, great seeker of the past and present. Now comes the one for whom we've waited. She alone has seen the warrior. She alone can release him."

Jo shivered. Nausea roiled in her stomach, the taste of bile bitter in her mouth. Something in the smoke was causing her head to spin. She leaned against Isobel, almost staggering, then felt a man's arm around her waist.

Rob's arm.

"What is this foolishness?" he growled. "I leave you alone for five minutes, and you're already in trouble."

"Trouble, yes, you are all in trouble," the old hag crooned. "As above, so below. There is no escaping the Nephilim."

Rob had had enough. While there was no doubt the gypsy woman was creepy, the Nephilim were the imaginings of the Old Testament, when people believed fallen angels slept with the women of Canaan and gave rise to a race of giants.

"There are no Nephilim, old woman," he said softly, then went to lead his wife from the tent before he realized she had slipped into a trance of some sort. Jo's eyes rolled back in her head, and she swayed to the sound of his voice.

The one-eyed gypsy hissed at him. "You, I've heard of you who call yourself doctor. What would you know of Nephilim—or Wendigos? One and the same, cursed and left to walk the earth forever."

Behind them, Isobel began to scream. "It's coming. Run, run!"

"Enough!" Rob roared.

The tent flap lifted, and Jason Cavendish raced in. He took one look at Isobel, who continued to scream, and slapped her hard.

The sound of her gasp startled everyone except the old woman, who had backed deep inside the tent, holding the crystal ball in the crook of her arm. "No matter the name, the future is the same. Death to all who disturb the Wendigo sleep." She slipped out of the tent, and just as quickly, Jo fell forward as Rob scooped her up in his arms.

He turned and stared at Isobel, his lips thin with anger. "What have you done? I knew we shouldn't have brought you back to the White Mountains. Is this how you repay Jo? What sort of sister are you?"

Isobel began to cry in earnest. "I didn't know what the gypsy would say. She told me to fetch my sister. Said she needed to talk with her. How did I know that crazy old bat would speak like that?"

"Don't pretend to care now, Isobel. We all know better." Rob slipped under the tent flap that Jason held for them, holding Jo in his arms. He glared at Isobel, then strode away, headed for their carriage. That one dark look spoke volumes.

Isobel squinted back tears. "Jason, you believe me, don't you? What did the gypsy tell you?" He pulled away from her, shaking her hand from his arm.

"Nothing. She said nothing." He strode after Rob as if his life depended on the doctor's presence.

Isobel stared at the young man's stiff back and swallowed her tears. What was the point of apologizing? She didn't owe Jason anything. Certainly not an explanation. No, this wasn't the first time a man had pushed her away. No doubt it wouldn't be the last. She'd been right from the beginning. She had no use for men.

CHAPTER FIVE

The mood at Miramar Hall was somber indeed. Jo still hadn't regained consciousness, though her eyes no longer rolled back in her head. However, Rob was unable to wake her and had given up on the usual remedies, like smelling salts.

Seated behind him, Arthur Cavendish cleared his throat. "Perhaps some brandy? Maybe we should call a doctor."

Rob turned and stared at the older man. So what if his expression revealed anger and disgust? For over an hour, Arthur had insulted not only his intelligence but also his ability. He *WAS* a doctor, for God's sake. Wasn't that why Arthur had wanted them to visit? To treat his son?

Arthur coughed and glanced away. "Sorry, Rob. Sorry! I wasn't thinking. Those damn gypsies. We need to drive them out of the county and not let them back next year."

Slightly mollified, Rob sighed and accepted the glass of brandy Arthur offered. "I thought you said the farmers around here need their help, their expertise with the crops."

"Yes, yes. But look what has happened."

"What exactly has happened, Arthur?" Rob sat down on the edge of Jo's bed, absently rubbing her palm. His wife was inside there, somewhere. He just needed to find her.

"The gypsy woman spoke of Wendigos," he continued. "I've never heard the term. But she spoke of Nephilim as well and said they were one and the same. And the other night you were talking about the Bible and gibberish about..."

Arthur sprang from the overstuffed chair in the corner of the room. "Wendigos? The gypsy spoke of Wendigos?" The usual ruddy color drained from the older man's face. "Why would she speak of such a thing? They aren't real." He began to pace the confines of the room, strangely keeping just to the edge of the oriental rug in the middle. Sort of like a child playing hopscotch; don't step on the crack, break your mother's back.

"Arthur, what is a Wendigo?" Rob asked quietly. He called on all his mesmerism skills at that moment. Jason was right. There was something very wrong in this household.

Arthur sank back into his easy chair, feet absently splayed in front. He began to rub his forehead, as though afflicted by a migraine. He closed his eyes and said, "Wendigos aren't real, Rob. They're Algonquin folklore."

"More Indian tales," Rob said dismissively, but in reality, he hoped to draw the older man out. Arthur was hiding something, and Rob had no idea what or why.

Arthur leaned forward, palms on his legs as he began to rhythmically rub his thighs. The motion apparently soothed him, for his expression changed, the corners of his eyes crinkling with amusement. "So, you haven't lost the touch, have you, Rob? You always did know how to provoke a man into giving up his deepest-held secrets."

A low moan from the bed captured Rob's attention. "Rob, is that you?" Jo whispered. "I saw the giant Indian again today."

"Where, Jo? Where did you see him?"

She slowly inched up in the bed, rubbing her eyes. "I feel like I've been sleeping for days," she said.

"Just a few hours, sweetheart. Where did you see the Indian?"

"In the gypsy tent. He was way in the back, crouched down, swaying back and forth on the balls of his feet. Why is he following me?"

"We'll find out, I'm sure." Rob grimaced as he rubbed her palm with his thumb. Her hand was as cold as ice. "Can you remember anything else?"

"I think he is trying to talk to me. To warn me about something. But where his mouth should be, there's just this huge red slash, like someone cut off his lips. It was quite horrible." Jo shivered violently. "Maybe we shouldn't have come here," she whispered, but the words were loud enough that Arthur heard them.

"Now, now. Not a word of it," the older man said, striding to the bedside. "You've been listening to Alison's bedtime stories. I'll see that she stops."

Rob cut him off. "Arthur, can you let Isobel and the others know that Jo is awake and appears fine? We'll see you all in the morning. Right now, I want her to get some real sleep."

Arthur appeared ready to argue, but Rob's lifted brow ended the discussion.

As soon as he'd left, Jo threw her arms around his neck. "I am so glad you're here," she said.

"Of course, I'm here. Where else would I be?" He drew her down onto his lap, nuzzling her neck. She needed to warm up.

"With Alison?" she whispered.

"Good God, Jo. Don't tell me you're jealous of that little twirp." He leaned back, looked into her eyes, then grinned. "You are jealous."

"A little, I guess," she admitted. "I never knew I could feel like this."

"Well, get such thoughts out of your head. There's only one woman for me." Determined to show her what he meant, he drew the comforter around them, but within minutes Jo was sound asleep. He would have to reassure her in the morning.

They woke to the sound of a bugle blowing.

Not just once or twice, but a full-blown, bloody rendition of "Taps." The mournful, melancholic notes cut through the early dawn just as the sun rose over Miramar Hall.

Rob raced down the long central staircase, his chest bare. He'd pulled on his trousers from the night before, telling Jo to stay in bed.

Arthur stood in the enormous open doorway to Miramar, hands on his hips.

"What the bloody hell is going on around here?" Rob yelled. "Who is playing the bugle and why? No one is being buried at dawn, are they?"

"Has it started again, Father?" Alison asked, standing behind them. Rob hadn't heard her approach.

"You mean this has happened before?" Rob said. From the corner of his eye, he noticed Isobel crouched beneath the stairwell, listening.

Alison looked from one man to the other. She had drawn a black woolen robe over her shoulders, but it hung loosely at her sides, and the white nightgown beneath appeared soiled at the hem, as though she'd been walking outdoors.

Rob grabbed her shoulder. "I asked you a question," he growled. "This craziness has to stop."

She pulled away, swallowing rapidly. "Yes, it has happened before. And yes, it is crazy." From the quaver in her voice, Rob realized she was close to tears.

"Why do you think Father sent my brother to fetch you?" she added. "Didn't Jason tell you?"

"Tell me what?"

"It would seem Miramar Hall is haunted," she replied, then simply walked away toward the kitchen. "I'm going to see what cook has left to eat from last night. I'm ravenous."

CHAPTER SIX

Rob watched as Alison scooped up a handful of sliced roast beef and began shoveling it into her mouth. Blood oozed from her lips.

"No ghost was playing that bugle this morning," he remarked. His words sounded much louder than he'd intended, echoing in the cavernous kitchen.

"Have some," she urged him.

"No thanks. I'm going to boil some eggs for Jo and myself. Isobel, would you like some?"

Isobel couldn't contain the shudder of revulsion that rolled over her shoulders. "I'm not hungry," she whimpered, staring at Alison in dismay. "Wouldn't you rather have a sandwich?" she asked Jason's sister.

"Oh, no. It's so much better like this." The dark-haired woman crammed more rare beef into her mouth, drops of blood running down her chin.

Arthur appeared oblivious to his daughter's actions. He paced the perimeter of the kitchen, this time stepping over the cracks between the enormous slabs of granite serving as the floor.

Rob poured cold water over a small pot of eggs and set them on the stove. "I've made some extra in case you change your mind,

Imp." He ruffled Isobel's curls, then mouthed "Ignore her" before turning back to the stovetop.

Isobel pulled up a stool and sat beside him, watching Arthur pace. "Should I get Jo up?" she whispered.

Rob shook his head. "I'll bring our eggs upstairs. Why don't you join us? We can talk."

Isobel nodded. Neither of them could escape the kitchen soon enough.

Just then, a blood-curdling shriek from upstairs broke the silence. "Watch the eggs," he ordered, then ran for Jo. He would recognize that scream anywhere.

She sat in the middle of their bed, a mound of pale blue nightgown and white sheets. On the floor lay their comforter. Jo pointed at it, hand to her mouth. As he bent to pick it up, he realized the floorboards were covered with bloody footprints.

Small bloody footprints.

Not a man's, for sure. Maybe a child's?

"What the hell!" He bent and touched one. Dry, almost powdery. They had to have been there when he went out first this morning. He ran right over them and never noticed. God! Was there blood all over his feet?

He sat on the bed next to Jo and lifted his bare feet to look at the soles. Not a drop of red. This morning was growing stranger by the minute. He remembered Alison's dirty nightgown. Why would she have gone outside in her nightclothes? Could she have been in their bedroom? For that matter, could she have blood on her feet? Maybe walked on her tiptoes around their room?

He would have answers today, or they would leave.

Isobel appeared at their bedroom doorway, holding a tray of eggs and tea. "Don't come in," Rob warned. "Stay in the sitting room, and we'll join you there."

Isobel looked down at the footprints on the floor, and her mouth formed an instantaneous moue, but she backed away without a word.

Rob lifted Jo in his arms and quickly left the bedroom. It would take the servants most of the morning to get those stains off the wood floor.

Assuming they still had servants.

He settled Jo on a chaise and began to peel the eggs.

"Want some help?" Isobel asked quietly.

"Sure, if you're going to eat?"

She grinned. "Yes, Dr. Radnor. My fasting days are over. But did you see Alison eat that beef? It was disgusting."

"This whole household is bizarre. I know we would enjoy the Glen House much more than this crazy place. I'm thinking maybe we should leave."

Isobel nodded in agreement. "How could Alison eat so much food and be so thin? After you left, she said she eats half a pound of roast beef every morning. How is that possible?"

Rob could only shake his head. Seemingly, anything was possible at Miramar Hall. Within minutes, their eggs were shelled, and Rob presented Jo with one, cuddled in a small porcelain cup.

"You did a good job, Imp. These are cooked perfectly," he said, and Isobel smiled.

"Who knew I would like to cook?" she replied. She began to cut up her own eggs, adding a pat of butter on top.

"Who indeed."

"Well, since I've met you, I've been putting on weight. If I had Alison's constitution, I could eat all day and not worry about it."

"Don't wish for something you might not really want."

Rob stretched and got to his feet. "I'm going to dress, and then I think we should all go downstairs and talk to Arthur. Will you both let me be the one to ask the questions?"

The women glanced at each other. Jo almost looked like she had something to say, then nodded instead. "Yes, Rob. I think that would be best. Don't you, Isobel?"

The younger woman agreed.

Once he'd left the sitting room, Isobel peeked behind the door to make sure he wasn't standing there. Satisfied, she turned to her sister.

"Jo, there is something wrong with Alison. She was cramming handfuls of roast beef, raw at that, into her mouth for breakfast."

"There is something wrong with this whole place," Jo replied.

"Oh, not with Jason. Surely, he is just overly concerned."

"No, Isobel. Jason didn't come to Boston to see Rob because he is all right."

"Yes, he did. Alison told us this morning that Arthur sent him to fetch Rob because there is something wrong with the house. That it is haunted."

"What? That is preposterous! Rob would never take on another challenge like more ghosts. Not after what happened at the Glen House. Have you forgotten we both almost died?"

"Keep your voice down, Jo. This is between us."

Just then, Rob walked in, casually dressed in a white cambric shirt and brown trousers. "Keeping secrets again, Imp. It never works out when you do."

Isobel stuck out her tongue. "And you were listening at the door, which you've told me not to do. So there."

Rob ruffled her hair and smiled. "We're even then. So what do you make of the footprints on our bedroom floor?" he asked.

Isobel backed away. "It wasn't me!" she yelled.

"I know. That was an honest question," he replied.

He knew the footprints were the sort of prank Mary and Isobel would have played on them when they were at the Glen House five years earlier. Only Mary lived with her brother now, who had since married and moved to the Midwest somewhere. No, this was something far more nefarious than child's play.

Isobel almost pouted as she sat on the bed next to Jo. "I don't know what to think," she said quietly. "They look like they'd been there a while. Didn't you lock the bedroom door last night?"

Rob shook his head. "I honestly don't know, Imp. I think I did, but Jo and I both fell asleep together, so I'm not sure. But the door was unlocked when I raced out this morning with that bugle blaring."

He looked at Jo for confirmation. She pensively pushed her hair back from her face and said, "I don't remember much about last night. Everything is sort of a blur. Sorry."

"Well, let's get you dressed and go downstairs. There has to be someone around here who can answer our questions."

CHAPTER SEVEN

The downstairs was completely empty, the front door still thrown wide.

The slab of roast beef sat on the kitchen countertop, covered with flies. Rob grabbed a pair of tongs and threw the meat out the back door.

"Is anyone here?" he yelled, tossing the tongs in the sink.

Just then, Annabelle, the head cook, sauntered in and placed her straw hat on the coat rack.

"What are you all doing in the kitchen?" the colored woman asked. "Didn't Alice make you breakfast?"

"Alice didn't come in today," Rob replied. "At least, we haven't seen her. We all awoke to the sound of a bugle playing taps. Would you happen to know anything about that?"

Annabelle finished putting on her apron and wiped her hands down the front. "If it was a bugle, then that would be the master's men."

"The master's men?" Rob quizzed. "Slavery went out with the war between the States."

"Mr. Arthur. He be the master here."

"Oh, right. So where would we find the master's men?"

"I imagine at the carriage house or the old privy. They been doing work down there."

After getting directions from Annabelle, they followed along an overgrown wooden walkway that led from the back kitchen door through a bramble of thorns and poison ivy that wound around huge tree trunks far above their heads. No one dared step off the walkway. Deep within the woods, shielded from the sun, the air smelled dank with rot and mold.

"These woods aren't anything like those around the Glen House," Isobel announced, cautiously peering down the pathway. "I wish we were there."

"That's because we are near the lake," Rob explained. "These woods have been here a long time, whereas many of those in the White Mountains have been logged at one time or another."

Jo sniffed. "I think you are idealizing again, Isobel. There are also plenty of reasons not to like the woods in the White Mountains. Like those on Mount Washington, for example. Have you forgotten I almost died up there? For that matter, running through the woods to the Emerald Pool?"

Isobel's cheeks turned bright pink. She didn't need a reminder of her sister and Dr. Radnor having sex on the banks of the Emerald Pool.

She marched ahead, and Jo smiled. Her sister hadn't matured that much.

Once she'd gone beyond earshot, Jo turned to Rob. "What do you think is really going on?"

He shook his head. "I honestly don't know. This place is as odd as the Glen House was when it was full of psychics. I feel just as nervous as I did then, also with good reason. Maybe we should send Isobel on to the Glen House. You too, for that matter."

Jo stopped and glared at him, and he was reminded why he loved her. She was valiant, steadfast, and magnificent, with her mahogany locks loose and curling around her waist. He smiled and put up his palm in truce. "Okay, maybe Isobel?"

Just then, her sister came racing back down the trail, features pinched, skin white as bleached bedsheets. "Oh my God," she whispered as she drew near. "The stench from up above is inhuman."

"Why are you whispering?"

"I don't want them to hear me."

"Who?"

"I don't know. Whoever it is that's digging."

"Digging?"

Isobel nodded. "Yes, digging."

"Can I leave the two of you here?" Rob asked.

"Not in this lifetime," the two women replied in unison.

"I'm not staying in these woods without a weapon," Isobel added.

Leave it to Isobel to add a little more drama.

Rob sighed. "Okay, Imp. But I want the two of you to stay behind me."

As they rounded the bend in the trail ahead, the smell indeed became insufferable, permeating the air to the point of gagging. He could only imagine the odor comparable to the roast beef he'd thrown outside earlier if it had been left to sit for a couple of weeks on the kitchen countertop.

Rob pulled out a handful of white kerchiefs from his trouser pockets and handed them to the women, folding one around the lower part of his own face. He'd taken to carrying them years ago during the war and had learned how handy they could be in a pinch.

Before long, they came to an overgrown clearing; the clink of shovels and grunting made it clear someone was digging. In the center of the clearing stood several outhouses in various degrees of neglect. The door from one looked near to falling off, and the roof of the other had completely caved in. Arthur Cavendish leaned against a doorframe, sweat running in rivulets down his face, along with traces of dirt. A thin, older man continued to dig in what had to be at least a four-foot-deep hole. He looked vaguely familiar, but Rob couldn't place why.

Next to Arthur's feet lay a wooden box, possibly pine, perhaps two feet square.

"Arthur, what are you doing?"

An utter look of horror flashed across his former captain's face, his gaze terrified as his eyes darted right to left and back again. He resembled a badger held at bay by a pack of hounds.

"We need to get what is left of this man into the ground immediately," Arthur ground out.

Rob stared down. There was no way that small box held a "man."

He motioned to the women to move ahead and approached his former friend. "What do you have there, Arthur?" he asked. "Can you tell us what is going on? Why can't this poor soul have a Christian burial in a churchyard?"

"Because he will become unholy soon."

Rob bent and lifted the top off the pine box, then gagged and almost threw up. Inside, a head covered in blood along with one torn-off arm lay on a battered gray Army blanket.

Suddenly Rob recalled why he knew the man digging the hole. After the war between the states, Arthur had been sent to arrest George Trenholm, treasurer of the Confederacy, who had been accused of stealing millions in assets. When Arthur returned, he brought back three southern men—"the captain's men," as they were called—who Arthur said turned coat on Trenholm and revealed that the entire Bank of Louisiana had been stolen by a Colonel Rice on Trenholm's behalf. As Rob recalled, the money had never been recovered.

"Your name is Wiley," he said, addressing the wizened gent standing in the hole. "One of the captain's men still, I see. Was this poor devil another?"

He turned to Arthur and grabbed the older man's shoulder. "I read the old Jesuit pamphlet in your library," he said quietly. "I know all about Wendigos now, Arthur. I've been asking you about them for days, hoping you'd tell me the truth. Don't you think some honesty is overdue?"

Arthur's sunken cheeks took on a ruddy hue, and he shrugged Rob's hand from his shoulder. "I don't answer to you or any man, for that matter. This is between me and my maker."

"You are wrong, Arthur. You invited me to come here under false pretenses. You lied and deceived me and have put all of us in danger." Rob's voice dropped, the words clipped and chill. "Now you will tell us what is going on, or we are leaving. Immediately."

Arthur's anger departed as quickly as it arrived. Completely deflated, he sank to the dirt in front of the privy. "If you leave now, we are all done for."

"Where did this Wendigo come from?" Rob asked. "How long has it been hunting in these woods?"

"How should I know? Perhaps forever. Perhaps since Chief Chocorua was driven to the mountaintop and jumped off. We became aware of it a couple of years after we dug up the giant Indian."

The old man named Wiley climbed out of the hole. "It wasn't you who dug that Injun up," he said, brushing dirt from the front of his trousers. "It was Harold and Sam and me. We hid the captain's gold in that grave, we did. Took out an iron trunk a year. Took our cut and went back home to Savannah. We just tucked the iron trunks amongst the bones and covered everything back up."

"So what happened to the Indian's head?"

"Weren't no head at that grave. Just scattered bones." Wiley picked at his one front tooth with a dirt-tinged fingertip, and Rob shuddered. God only knew what contamination just entered the man's mouth. "Then a few years ago we went to the grave to dig it back up, and it was already turned over. Someone looking for our gold, only didn't seem any trunks was missing. Not 'til the other night when we did the captain's bidding and discovered there was only one trunk left."

"So who is this poor soul?" Rob asked, pointing to the open box.

"Oh, that be Harold," Wiley said matter-of-factly. "I found him this morning down behind the carriage house, or what was left of him. Played taps as befitted a military man, then cobbled together that box out of some wood scraps the captain found."

Rob nodded. "And what has become of Sam?" he asked.

"Ain't seen Sam in days, not since the captain paid us."

Rob turned to his friend. "Arthur, why do you think there is a Wendigo involved? Why couldn't it just be the gypsies digging for your gold, putting the fear of God into you to keep you from looking in that grave?"

Arthur stared at him for a minute. Was that a glimmer of hope in the man's pale green eyes? "I suppose it is possible. Gypsies all along." The older man crawled to his feet, brushing off the dirt from his trousers.

"But my daughter, Alison. Why is she acting so odd?" he muttered. "It's why I sent Jason to fetch you here."

"Probably because of all the wild tales you've been telling each other at night. If I stayed cooped up at Miramar Hall day after day, I'd go mad myself. You need to go out, meet people, and get involved in things in the community."

Arthur's face once again grew dark with anger. His small eyes darted back and forth. "What about the gold? I can't let anyone know about it. People will steal it from me, just like they did from the grave."

Rob began to wonder about Arthur's sanity. The man was consumed by greed, by the gold he'd stolen from George Trenholm. No good could ever come from stolen riches, even if it did come from the Confederacy.

He walked over to Wiley and took the shovel from the older man.

"Would you have some salt in the carriage house?" he asked, climbing into the hole and beginning to dig. "From what I've read, the body parts need to be salted and burned before burying."

Then he looked at Arthur over the edge of the grave and smiled. "Not that I believe in Wendigos. Just in case," he added before going back to digging. "No reason not to cover all our bases."

CHAPTER EIGHT

By midafternoon, they found Jason working on another landscape. He was up on the bluff overlooking the pond, seated before his easel on an upended wooden crate bearing a label stating FRESH PLUMS. His eyes looked sunken and tired; his unshaven chin darkened by a day's growth.

He hurriedly turned the canvas around as they approached.

Overhead, an ancient oak threw the only shade, beneath which wild blackberries grew in abundance, throwing off the summer's first fruit.

"Have you been out here all night?" Rob asked while Jo and Isobel began picking berries and eating them.

"I saw it last night and needed to capture the image," Jason replied, looking at the ground.

"Saw what?"

"You know. The ghost." He sighed and turned the canvas back around. Once again, he'd drawn the pond below, but this time on the shore hovered a dark, amorphous cloud, whirling like a small tornado.

"Ah, yes. The ghost. And you think it lives out here?"

"Sure of it." Jason pointed to the ridge directly opposite them on the other side of the pond. "I've lived here my entire life and never noticed that stone outcropping before. Not until this morning. When the sun comes up, it illuminates the whole ridge. There must be mica in that granite, and it began to flicker and gleam. And then I saw the ghost for a second time."

"What did you see, Jason?"

"Fast, really fast." The younger man shuddered. "Like a black blur. Huge. Then it stopped and looked right at me. Sunken eyes that glowed with an eerie yellow light. Its mouth opened, and this long, dark blue tongue emerged, flicked once or twice, and then it was gone. Just like that. A blur of motion. Gone."

A low moan emitted from Jason's lips. "We are so screwed."

"Well, that's one way of putting it," Isobel said, popping another ripe blackberry in her mouth.

"That's enough, both of you." Rob began to pace. "What you saw was no ghost, Jason. Ghosts don't lick their lips or stick out their tongues, for that matter. No, I think that was a Wendigo."

"Oh, God. So now you believe in it also."

"I never said I didn't believe in it, Jason. Your father has denied their existence since we arrived. But he owns books that clearly describe them, treatises from the 1600s from settlers all the way to Canada who encountered the creatures."

Jo and Isobel sank down on the grass, eating berries from Jo's wide-brimmed straw hat. "So what is a Wendigo?" Jo asked, her words sounding remarkably calm.

"That's the million-dollar question, sweetheart. From what I've gathered so far, a Wendigo is one of two things. It is either a monster with some human characteristics, or it is an evil spirit, a demon who has possessed a human being and made them monstrous."

Jason turned to face them. "Like I said, a ghost."

"No, Jason. No offense, but we three have dealt with ghosts in the past, and ghosts don't hurt you. Right, Isobel?"

The young woman met his gaze, then smiled. "Right. Like Billy, at the Glen House. He played games with us and tried to trick us, but he never actually hurt us."

"That is correct, Imp. Because a ghost is just a memory of a person; it isn't capable of physical harm. Though you have to be careful of their pranks and not hurt yourself by believing everything they tell you."

"No, I'm leaning more towards a demon," he continued. "One who has possessed a human. It would explain why they are so long-lived. So malevolent. Demons are ever greedy. No matter how much they get, they want more. So the demon starts off eating dogs or cats or mice and rats, then moves on to humans. The more it eats human flesh, the more it wants."

Isobel shuddered. "Like Alison?" she whispered.

Rob nodded. "Quite possibly."

Jason jumped to his feet. "See, I told you my sister wants my brain."

Rob smiled. "Apparently in more ways than I imagined."

Jo slapped his arm. "Stop joking around. This is awful, Rob. What are we going to do? Perhaps you are right, and we should leave."

"We can't leave now. At least I can't. What would happen to Arthur, to the rest of them?"

Jo's lips thinned, and she shook her head. "It's always about everyone else but us."

"Sister! That's not true. Rob has helped us tremendously," Isobel interrupted. "I mean, I learned how to eat food again. Real food."

Jo sighed and looked down into her lap. "I can't fight you both."

Rob squatted down and took her hands in his. "Jo, no one wants to fight with you. We're in this together. I love you, remember?" The corners of his chocolate-brown eyes crinkled as he smiled at her, and Jo felt her heart thump erratically. It had always been this way, from the first day she met him at his office in Boston. He had some magical, very irritating way of making her forget what her point was.

"You are an infuriatingly handsome man, but that still doesn't get you off the hook," she said, coming to her feet.

Rob smiled, a twinkle in his eye. "Isobel, can you and Jason go for a walk? Not too far; just so Jo and I can have a few minutes."

Isobel's lips formed a moue, but she grabbed Jason's hand and pulled him toward the pond. "Let's go see if we can find some frogs."

"Let's not!" he exclaimed, pulling his hand free. "I hate slimy things. Let's just look at the birds, and I'll teach you how to skip rocks."

Once they were alone, Rob gave his wife a hug. "So, Jo," he said, taking his time to find the right words, "I've been thinking that I owe you an apology. When we were at the Glen House five years ago and I thought you'd died, I swore to myself I would never put you in danger again."

Jo made to speak, but he put his hand up. "Let me finish, please. I know you didn't ask me to keep you safe. We never talked about it. I guess we should have. Because I find myself in a dilemma now."

"All right. Explain."

"I've been thinking about time."

Jo grinned but held her tongue. Only Rob would think about such a mundane thing.

"Time is the most elusive commodity of all," he continued. "We only get so much of it, and I fear I've wasted the past five years just trying to keep you both safe. I've also realized I'm bored out of my mind. I don't want the same boring patients with the same old boring complaints."

He ran his fingers through his thick brown hair and grinned a little sheepishly. "I need my old life back."

"I've wondered why you'd stopped hunting down quacks," she said. "And you're right; we stopped talking months ago, maybe even years. You come home from your office, and we all eat dinner. Then you go into your study every night 'to work,' and Isobel and I go upstairs to the sitting room to read. Then I go to bed and toss and turn all night, wondering why you don't come to me. Lately I've been getting up and writing down our exploits. I might as well do something since I can't sleep."

"What? When?"

"Months ago. Isobel and I have been reading Dickens. We had just finished *The Haunted Man*, and Isobel said to me, 'Sister, we could write something better than this. We could call it *The Emerald Pool*.' I thought about what she said that night and got up and started writing."

"That's wonderful, Jo. You should have told me."

"Like I said, we never talk anymore."

"I didn't want to potentially put you or Isobel in danger. I figured we were married, and it was time to settle down," he explained.

Jo threw herself at Rob. "And all this time I've been thinking you had someone else on the side. Isobel told me that men do that sometimes, take a mistress." Her fingers grabbed the back of his neck as she drew his head down for a kiss. His response held nothing back, his tongue plunging into her mouth, twining with hers.

In a few minutes, he drew away and coughed. "It has been a long time since we made love. However, I had to remind myself just now that Isobel and Jason are with us." His words sounded tremulous, and Jo smiled gently as he smoothed down the front of his trousers.

"No repeat of the Emerald Pool?" she said, laughing, and he grinned back.

"Not this afternoon. But the night awaits."

"So, finish what you were saying."

"Oh, yes. I've been thinking about Lumina. We never discussed what happened. Not really."

"I thought she was my friend," Jo said quietly, twisting a lock of her dark red hair. "Turned out it was all an act."

Rob shook his head. "I believe in some ways she was a friend to both of us. But her soul had become possessed, consumed by that damned necklace. The Eye of Horus had her in its clutches and eventually killed her."

"But I thought Dr. Burgess..."

"Oh, he controlled Mary and used her to perform Lumina's execution, but Mary was just a pawn, as was Dr. Burgess. Ultimately, the Eye of Horus was in control of everything. If Isobel hadn't thrown the Eye into the Emerald Pool, I doubt any of us would have survived."

He took a deep breath. "I believe Alison is under a similar type of control," he continued. "A Wendigo, for lack of a better word. A demon."

Jo grinned. "And you're afraid I have a sign around my neck saying, 'All demons welcome here?'" she replied.

Laughter burst from Rob's lips, and he swung Jo in his arms. "I know better now," he said. That was how Jason and Isobel found them as they climbed back up to the top of the hill, dragging a piece of wet cloth behind them.

A torn, red-stained bedsheet. On it, written in black paint, were the words: HELP ME.

CHAPTER NINE

"I think we need to go back to the Indian grave," Jo remarked. "Most of him is missing, but there might be a clue still remaining."

They'd returned to Miramar Hall to show Arthur and his daughter the sheet, only to discover the house in an uproar. Arthur had invited guests for dinner and never informed the staff or anyone but the invited guests. From the kitchen, Annabelle could be heard yelling at the kitchen help, clearly angry at the unexpected, last-minute preparations. No one had seen Alison, nor did Arthur appear to care. "She'll show up when she wants," he said. "It's not like this hasn't happened before."

"Arthur, we need to talk about what *has* happened," Rob interrupted.

Arthur dismissively waved a hand at him. "What's happened? Nothing has happened. I've guests arriving, and the last thing they want to hear about is old Indian legends." Arthur clapped Jason on the back. "There's money to be made, son. These are people with real money, and I have a proposition for them. I'm going to get that last spur of the Algonquin Railroad built, by hook or crook. Get that? Hook or crook?"

Jason's upper lip lifted in disgust. "Don't we have enough money, father?"

Arthur wheeled on them both. "What a ridiculous thing to say. There's never enough money. You should know that. I brought you up better, for all the good it's done. All you want to do is paint pretty pictures. How is that going to pay the bills? Huh?"

Jason turned to leave, but Rob grabbed his shoulder. "Don't run," he whispered. "Stand your ground."

Jason swallowed, then nodded and turned back to his father. "Someday, those pretty pictures will sell for thousands, father. When they do, I hope you're still alive to apologize."

As they walked away, Jo said, "Well, that came as quite a shock. Has your father always been such a nasty man?"

Jason looked like he might cry, but he shook his head. "No, not really. He was always strict and very controlling, but he used to tell me to explore, to think about what I wanted to do in the world. To try different things until I felt comfortable with one of them. Just because I'm still not sure, well, I certainly didn't expect him to attack me like that."

Rob pulled on Jason's arm, and they all stopped for a minute. "So, when Arthur sent you to Boston to see me, along with his invitation, did he tell you what the trip was really for?" Rob asked.

"I understood he wanted you to visit to find out what was wrong at the house. To figure out why Alison is acting so weird, so aggressive."

"So your father never mentioned he believed Miramar Hall was haunted?"

"No, never. Why would you say that?"

"Because Alison told us you were sent to Boston because the house was haunted and your father needed me to rid the place of ghosts."

Jason simply stared at him, then shook his head. "That's ridiculous. There's never been any mention of the house being haunted."

"So why were you dressed in disguise when you came to Boston?" Isobel asked.

"Because father said he didn't want anyone to know we had problems. Why else would people go to the doctor? Certainly not because everything was fine."

"And Arthur suggested the disguise?"

"Yes, said he didn't want anyone knowing I was seeing a doctor of the mind."

"A doctor of the mind, hmm. That's one way to put it."

They walked on to the stables, where Rob asked one of the hands to bring Arthur's carriage around. They all climbed in, throwing several shovels and a pickaxe on the back floor.

Jo and Isobel had both changed into trousers before leaving Miramar Hall earlier in the day to find Jason, and Jo had borrowed a woolen shirt from Rob's closet. With their hair pulled up beneath slouch hats, neither would have been mistaken for women, which was the whole idea. No need for the neighbors to know they'd gone out to explore.

"Just keep your heads down if anyone asks, and I'll handle things," Rob ordered as they pulled away in the carriage. "We're just digging for worms; doing a little fishing."

Jo started to laugh, but his words did make sense, not that they would probably meet anyone. Persons of note were probably dressing for Arthur's dinner while the rest boated on the lake in the late afternoon sun.

"We'll need to get back in time to dress for dinner," Jo reminded him.

"I know. This won't take long."

In less than an hour, they approached the bend in the gravel road turning toward Melvin Village. They hadn't seen a soul.

"We'll pull over here," Rob said, guiding the horses into the shade.

Jason squinted against the bright sunlight. "This is where you saw the gypsy boy?"

"Yes, over there." Rob pointed his cane toward the oak trees as he descended from the carriage.

Jason came around the back. "What a curious cane," he remarked, staring at Rob's fist. "I don't remember seeing it before now."

Isobel began to giggle. "I would say possessed. Not curious."

Rob glanced at Isobel, then smiled. "I'd say alive, not possessed."

"And I'd say none of us really know, including Rob." Jo stroked the ebony wolf's head, and Boromar winked at her. "See what I mean?"

Jason backed away, lips pursed. "How did you come by such a thing? Clearly it is evil."

Rob smiled at the younger man. "Boromar is hardly evil; quite the opposite. But there's nothing wrong with being afraid, Jason. I felt much the same when I left England, chasing after my older brother's fiancée."

"You were involved with her?" the younger man remarked.

Rob laughed. "God, no. Now you sound like my brother. No, she'd stolen some of our family's prized jewels and taken a ship to America. I was perhaps five years older than you are now and still in search of myself. Our father gave me Boromar as a parting gift."

Jason drew a little nearer and looked closely at Boromar's ivory shaft, his eyes squinched up as he peered at the cane's strange carvings. Rob continued, "I made it to the California gold fields and thought I wanted to be a surgeon. But after the war between the states, all the death, the mental anguish, I knew I'd been mistaken. I really wanted to help the soldiers who had survived."

"To help their minds, you mean?"

"Yes, but I quickly learned there are too many quacks in the medical field. We are not regarded well in the press either, and rightly so. In order to protect those soldiers who needed real help, I began to debunk the frauds and fakes that preyed on them. And here I am."

Clearly, Rob had left out a few parts, but Isobel listened to his story spellbound. "You never really told us about your past," she said. "At least not me."

Jo slipped her arm around her sister's waist. "He talked to me about Boromar, some of the family jewels, Isobel. Not much more, and I didn't ask."

"I should have told you both a long time ago. Yes, Boromar was one of my father's prized possessions. Much like your father, Jason, my wealthy father was also consumed by money. By possessions."

"So you inherited your money," Jason said quite plainly, as only an American could.

"No, actually I'm a self-made man, Jason. To inherit my father's estate, I'd have to return to England and accept all the responsibilities that would go along with his title. I decided not to pursue it, though I didn't tell my older brother my real plans. There's no harm done. I haven't seen or spoken with my brother Jericho in many years."

Once again, Jason took a step back, this time staring at Rob in obvious fascination. "Even in New England, we've heard of Jericho Radnor. Isn't he running for governor someplace out west?"

"Could be," Rob said. A smile flirted across his firm lips. "That wouldn't surprise me. So, let's go find what remains of our Indian, quite literally."

Despite their apprehension, it turned out there was little digging to be done. No one had filled in the hole. Pretty much hidden beneath the trees, with years of leaves on the ground, the grave remained open to the elements and appeared much the same as when they'd left it several weeks earlier.

Except, after looking around, they realized one thigh bone was missing. The same one Jo could have sworn moved on its own the day they found the grave. The same one the gypsy boy held in his hand before throwing it into the grave and running away.

Also, the quiver of arrows had been tossed onto the ground, where it lay partially covered by oak leaves. The silver-tipped arrows sparkled in the broken sunlight drifting through the oak tree branches.

"Do you think it's safe to touch them?" Isobel asked, kicking away the crinkled brown leaves with her boot.

"What, the leaves or the arrows?" Rob joked.

"Ha! Ha!" she quipped back. "The leaves, of course."

Rob drew on a pair of dark leather gloves. "I'll pick up the quiver and see if it looks safe."

Jason came to Jo's side. "Is she usually so fearless?"

"I'm afraid so. It's usually one extreme or the other with my sister."

He sighed. "I was afraid you'd say that."

"If you're interested in my sister, you will need to learn much from my husband. Isobel attracts all manner of things."

She left Jason to mull over what she'd meant. Rob had begun to slowly pull the silver-tipped arrows from the rotting leather quiver. The arrows appeared new, as though dipped in molten silver the night before. The only silver she was familiar with tarnished constantly and required a great deal of polishing. Why did these remain so bright?

Rob looked up at her, his brown eyes shining. A grin flitted across his lips. "Jo, what if we have it all wrong? Maybe this isn't the grave of the Wendigo, but of a great hunter. A Wendigo hunter."

"While his quiver has rotted, not his weapons?" queried Isobel. She took one of the arrows from Rob's fingers, turning it over in examination. "How curious. Look at this little silver band. It looks like it holds the arrowhead on. And something is written on it. Can you make it out, Rob?" Isobel jumped up and down with excitement.

"Your eyes are better than mine, Imp. I didn't even notice the band."

"But we don't have his bow. How would you shoot the arrows?" asked Jo.

"When you saw the Indian, did he have a bow?" Rob replied.

"Yes, he was holding it in his right hand. I told you that."

"Oh, I forgot. But this skeleton has no hand or finger bones, so perhaps whoever buried him here took the bow."

"We could make a bow," Jason said softly, peering into the grave. "I think we have a book about making weapons in the library. And our neighbor, Jim Sayers, shoots a crossbow. Perhaps he might have a regular bow we could borrow. I'll ask him tonight. I'm sure Father has invited him."

"Oh, my God," Jo burst out. "We need to get going. I need a bath, and dinner is in several hours."

"I know," Rob replied. "Isobel, can you help me gather up these arrows? I need to take a look at the inscription on that silver band you noticed. There must be a reason why it was put there."

CHAPTER TEN

Back in their suite at Miramar Hall, Rob pulled out a magnifying glass and held up the arrow so he could examine the silver band holding the arrowhead in place. Up close, the wooden arrow itself appeared ancient, the wood dull and scratched in places. But the silver band shone like the silver-tipped arrowhead, appearing brand new. Originally, he'd thought the band had been stamped, which would have made it of much newer manufacture than the quiver—or the bones, for that matter. Some sort of trick, perhaps. He had many doubts about everything they had experienced since arriving at Miramar Hall. But as he tried to make out the markings, he gasped and drew back.

Anasazi. How was that possible? The ancient people of the Bible who existed long before the birth of Christ. Yet their symbols existed to this day. Signs of protection. Others of birth, death, and immortality. What did these have to do with the Wendigo?

He looked closer at the symbols on the silver band. Strange circles with legs that looked like spiders without heads. A snail and various stick figures, along with the sun. A prominent sun throughout.

Rob felt out of his element. He hadn't really studied Anasazi, believing it an obsolete language. Who would have known he'd need it now? He had no idea what the symbols meant.

The hair on the back of his neck rubbed against his shirt collar, reminding him to shave. Oh, to hell with shaving. Arthur hadn't told them this morning that they would be having guests; they could live with his day's growth.

He pulled off his shirt, wondering how to protect the women he loved. He began to pace the chamber. On the other side of the door separating their rooms, he heard Jo talking with Isobel as she dressed. No doubt Imp was eager to head down for dinner. Him, not so much. Why did they keep running into such dangerous situations? Why had he ever agreed to come here?

He knew the answer. But his fear for Jo had his heart thudding in his chest... and so far... well, nothing much had really happened. Other than them finding the Indian grave.

He went back to look at the arrows strewn on his bed. They all had the same silver band on the neck. He pulled a clean shirt over his head, then looked for his pocket knife. At least there was something he could try.

Rob looked so darkly handsome Jo had to pinch herself to remember she was married to the man. He hadn't really dressed for dinner, but wore an off-white cambric shirt open at the collar, more suited for a picnic than a formal meal. She shrugged, smoothing down the front of her emerald green gown and hid a smile. A doctor of the mind could do most anything he wished.

Why Rob had chosen her for his wife was still a source of amazement. Five years of marriage and she still couldn't comprehend his desire for her. It wasn't her money; Rob had plenty of his own. There were so many beautiful women vying for his attention, yet his eyes always turned to her. Even tonight, though he made the usual small talk, several beautiful women, including Alison, leaned on his shoulder or paused just so to show off their bosoms. He nodded at something Alison said, then his gaze caught Jo's own, and he smiled. Just a brief little grin. A secret between the two of them. Though he spoke with Alison, he was mentally undressing his wife right there in the dining room.

Jo felt her nipples harden with desire. God, he was beautiful. More beautiful than any human had a right to be.

And he was all hers.

Alison's dark hair glistened in the gaslight, offset by the aquamarine gown she wore with casual ease.

Jo looked down at her own emerald dress and sighed. She'd worn the same dress at the Glen House five years ago. What was she thinking? She needed a new gown and had money to buy five hundred, but walked around like a pauper.

"Sister, you are a hundred times more attractive than Alison. Stop fidgeting."

"Am I that obvious?"

"To me, you are. But don't worry. No one is watching you. Except your husband, of course. He hasn't taken his eyes off you all night."

Jo sighed again. "Rob is so sinfully handsome, isn't he?"

Isobel glanced across the room to where Jason talked with a man she didn't recognize. "Actually, I like my men more refined. Your husband looks downright heathenish tonight."

"He does, doesn't he."

Isobel grinned. "I see you're wearing the ring he fashioned for you."

"And you the little charm he made. It's quite cute on that silver chain. I haven't seen it before."

Isobel cupped the silver charm in her palm and examined it carefully. "Jason gave me the necklace to hang it from. I don't know how much good the charm will do, but both Rob and Jason feel better with us wearing them."

"I wish we knew what the symbols meant."

Anasazi. Who'd ever heard of such a thing? Jo looked at the narrow silver band on her right pinkie finger. The only symbol she recognized was the sun. But the ring felt warm around her finger, as though it belonged there.

Rob would figure it out, he always did. And she couldn't deny she felt a tad safer wearing the trinket.

He had called it an amulet. "It will repel evil forces," he told her. "Such as those accompanying a curse. Think of it as your shield."

She stared at the ring hanging from the silver chain around her sister's neck. Rob had told them it was a talisman. Meant to attract good luck and repel demons.

Jo began to think she would have preferred a talisman herself. A sword was always better than a shield.

She noticed Isobel's wine glass was empty. "I hope you haven't had too much to drink," she remarked and took a sip of the madeira that Arthur had poured for the women after they'd all finished dinner. Apparently, Arthur didn't believe in the women retiring to the sitting room while the men talked politics. Which was fine. She had no desire to speak with Alison.

"It's kind of sweet, not like the wine we usually drink," Isobel said.

"That's because it is madeira, all the way from the Madeira Islands off the coast of Africa." Jo caught herself just before she said something stupid, like *We can't afford wine from Africa.* They could afford wine from Antarctica, if such a thing existed, which she sincerely doubted. Her mind raced along, fanciful thoughts dashing from one sentence to another.

"Jo, stop. You are giving me a headache." Jo just stood there for a second, dumbfounded. She hadn't been aware she'd been speaking out loud.

"Maybe you're the one who's had a little too much to drink," her sister said, then frowned and walked away. Rob came to her side and handed her another goblet of madeira, though she shook her head.

"Two glasses won't hurt, Jo. You need to loosen up and enjoy yourself a little."

Now it was Jo's turn to frown. Was Rob criticizing her? "I have some ideas on how we could enjoy ourselves," she said, taking his arm and putting down her glass while she led him outside onto the enormous stone veranda that encircled the house.

Hand-hewn from blocks of granite, the veranda surrounded Miramar Hall like a moat. Whip-poor-wills called from the lilac bushes that enveloped the walkways. In the spring, the dense, rich odor of the lilacs would permeate the air, mingled with the smell of iris.

Hundreds of cicadas trilled into the night, the sound deafening as they sang their song of desire and mating, of defeat and longing.

Rob pulled her close, his cambric shirt prickling her cheek. His face blocked out the moon as his warm lips brushed over her mouth, her chin, and the side of her neck.

Jo moaned with desire as he cupped her breast and gently pinched her nipple, which strained against the bodice of her dress. Her silk skirt rustled in the night air, sensuous and enticing.

Rob's words sounded harsh. "We need to go upstairs."

Jo began to mention saying their good nights, but Rob slipped his palm across her mouth and whirled her back to his chest, his arm holding her like a vise. He breathed in the aroma of her hair, the scent of lilac perfume. "If we don't go upstairs, I will take you right here, and be damned who sees."

He felt Jo's little intake of breath against his palm and the slight tremor of excitement as her legs gave out beneath her. Swooping her up in his arms, he stepped into the black inkiness of the night and disappeared up the outside stairwell.

What seemed like hours passed as Jo climaxed for him, and then again. While she had always been a little demanding and never shy in bed, tonight she seemed like a woman possessed. "It's the madeira," she mumbled several times.

"I'll order a case," he whispered into her mouth, then shuddered as she softly nibbled at the tip of his tongue. Her eager fingers latched onto his penis and drew him deep inside, crying out as he filled her.

"Oh God, Jo. Not so fast. I want to last," but no sooner did he say the words than ejaculate spilled from him.

Then he stilled. "Christ, Jo. I didn't put on a condom."

"That's all right," she whispered, bringing his hand down to rub against her swollen clitoris. "Can't you feel how much I want you again?"

"Jo, I'll be damned if you'll get pregnant after saying you don't want children. I thought we agreed? You need to be sober to make a decision like this."

She sighed softly. "Rob. Make love to me again." At that point, he gave up on talking.

Hours later, Rob pulled himself from the bed, poured several fingers of whiskey, and wandered onto the outside balcony. The cicadas had given up their noisy dance. The night appeared shrouded in secrecy, the woods surrounding the house eerily quiet. Clouds scattered over the face of the moon, long fingers streaking into the night sky.

Exhausted, Rob had been unable to sleep. He shook his head and gazed at the near-full moon, then took another sip of Glen Livet. What an idiot. If Jo got pregnant from this one stupid night of passion, what would they do?

As if they didn't have enough going on in their lives.

Pregnancy was one of the few things they had discussed at length in the past five years. Jo was fifteen years his junior and had every right to want children. But she had insisted from the beginning that she had no desire for babies of her own.

"Raising Isobel has been enough," she said. "I want to live my life with you. Not you and others."

Which made what had happened tonight so unusual that he couldn't wrap his mind around it. Jo usually took the lead and slipped a condom on his penis faster than he could stroke it. Tonight, she'd been oblivious. And because of her urgency, he had quite forgotten everything, which was no excuse.

"Damn it!" The night breeze gobbled the words up and danced away in merriment. Abortion was incomprehensible. Some of the midwives who practiced their arts were legitimate, but many were not. He would not risk Jo's life by sacrificing the child's.

But then, it wasn't really up to him, was it?

Sweat ran down his chest. How had things come to this?

Swish...swish. The soft sound repeated.

Rob walked to the balcony edge and looked down. Alison danced on the sweeping stone veranda below, head thrown back, eyes closed.

Impossible.

Who guided her?

As she turned in a pirouette, arms outstretched with the moon behind her, he glimpsed a shadowy figure of her moonlit lover—an immense, ghastly creature that whirled her around and around. It stared up at Rob with sunken, yellow eyes and grinned from the remnants of tattered lips.

This then, was the Wendigo.

The sound of blood whooshed in Rob's ears. His mouth went dry. Just then, he realized how desperately he needed to save them all.

Jo's voice called out, and he quietly walked backward into their room and shut the balcony doors—not before giving a little prayer, even for their unborn baby, should Jo be pregnant.

For Alison, he felt only pity. There could be no help for her. Only prayers for her undead soul.

CHAPTER ELEVEN

Jo rolled over and moaned, then smothered her head with a pillow. Why did she drink so much last night? Sunlight streamed through the balcony doors, bringing an ache to her eyes. How much *did* she drink? The entire night was a blur, except for Rob. She would never forget Rob's hands last night, or the depth of his passion.

Mortified, Jo struggled to sit up. Her cheeks burned just thinking of how many times they made love, had sex, whatever you called last night. Maybe crazy. It certainly hadn't been normal.

She looked about their bedroom, everything in place except her clothing. Her dress lay on the floor where she'd dropped it in her haste to have sex. Rob was nowhere in sight, and she was completely naked. Drawing up her knees, Jo realized how sore her legs were. Plus, she ached down there, in her private places. Little dots of blood speckled the sheets. What the hell!

Then Jo sighed as she realized her courses had started. How embarrassing. Perhaps that was the source of all her passion last night—hormones.

She quickly slipped off the edge of the bed and went to the traveling case on the bureau where she kept her cotton rags for such monthly occurrences. She pulled a white chemise over her head, then slipped a petticoat over the chemise. Rob came in just as she finished washing her hands.

He looked a little sheepish but came up and kissed the top of her head. "About last night," he said, but she shushed him.

"My courses came during the night," she said, "so blame it all on me. Or hormones."

"I thought it was the madeira?"

"Well, maybe a combination of both."

"Thank God, Jo." He drew her so close she could barely breathe.

"What is it?" she asked.

"You don't remember? We didn't use a condom."

"Oh. No. I don't remember much except your exquisite hands." She blushed deeply then and kissed him back. "I think you may have been a conductor in a previous life."

Rob laughed. "Right, a maestro."

"Well, you played my song last night, that's for sure."

He leaned into her, waiting for his heart to steady. "I couldn't sleep all night worried about a baby," he whispered.

He breathed in the scent of her.

Should he tell her about Alison?

No. She and the others would learn soon enough.

"Let's get some breakfast, slug-a-bed. There must be someone else up by now."

Only, when they went downstairs, no one was about. A green damask-covered divan had been dragged into the center of the hallway, a woman's black cloak draped over the back.

Rob could smell bacon and breakfast sausage. They walked into the long dining room and saw the mahogany sideboard laden with silver-plated servers. Jo immediately poured some tea and dropped in several sugar cubes, guzzling the tea like the most precious of waters.

"God, I can't believe how thirsty I am," she said, then took another sip.

"Me too," Isobel exclaimed, entering the room on Jason's arm. "I woke in the night and couldn't find my water pitcher. I went and stole Jason's," she added, smiling up at him shyly.

Jo just looked at them both.

Jason squirmed a little beneath the inquisitive stare. "We wondered if we could speak with you," he murmured. "Isobel and I have been awake most of the night talking and have come to an agreement."

"Can I get some coffee first?" Rob walked over to the coffee tureen, wondering how Jo was going to take the news. He was pretty sure more than just talking had occurred between Isobel and Jason. Moreover, he was beginning to think Jo was right about the madeira last night.

Isobel's eyes gleamed with merriment, but she demurely sat next to Jason on the overstuffed couch against the far wall and sipped on a cup of tea. Jo refilled her own cup and went to the long windows overlooking the front lawns, completely ignoring the other couple. Rob sighed and pulled up an oak dining room chair across from them and sat down.

"So, what did you want to talk about?"

Jason cleared his throat several times while Isobel just watched him curiously. Finally, the younger man said, "I'd like to take Isobel away from here."

"He's worried about me," Isobel explained, nodding her head. "His sister's not right in her mind. We saw her walking naked last night, out on the lawn. She tore at her hair like someone possessed and threw long bunches of it on the grass. Then she took off running and disappeared into the woods."

Jo continued to stare out the window, her back turned towards them, stiff as a rod. Rob knew she'd heard every word.

He cleared his thoughts. "I believe your sister is possessed, Jason. By the Wendigo. You are correct that it is not safe here, but we can't run away. It would just follow us."

"It isn't trapped here?" Jason exclaimed.

"I wish. No, I believe it is free to travel wherever it wants. That would explain why there are reports of seeing the creature throughout much of Canada and the upper United States. I mean, how many of them can there be? It may return here for food. Maybe the food is stored in that cave you thought you saw on the ridge."

Isobel shuddered. "That is so gross. Like it hibernates here in the winter and eats body parts?"

Jason ignored her comments. "So how do we help my sister?" His whispered words held a tinge of desperation.

Rob stared down at his own palms, hating the truth. "I don't believe there is help for your sister," he finally said, looking the younger man straight in the eye. "If we defeat the Wendigo, she might survive. But we will need to kill the creature and I'm not sure how to do that. It will require all my skills as a mesmerist and much more. And I will need help in order to set a trap."

While he wanted to talk to Jason about the young man's plans for the future, he decided to wait. He doubted Jason would lie to him. And it was obvious the younger man cared for Isobel. He still held on to her hand as though grasping a lifeline. Perhaps she represented exactly that.

"I talked with Jim Sayers last night," Jason continued. "He doesn't own a bow, but he said I could borrow one of his crossbows. He has several."

"That's great, Jason. Could you send him a note with one of the servants? In the meantime, we need to find that cave. I don't believe the creature can travel during daylight. So we will have to plan accordingly and all stay together at night for protection."

With that, Jo finally turned towards them. "That is the most sensible thing you've said, Rob. Safety in numbers. And no more wine. I don't know what kind of games Arthur is playing, but something was wrong with that madeira last night."

As though she had been listening from the doorway, Annabelle entered the room, whistling. She appeared to have never gone home, her once-white apron as dirty as the night before.

"Mr. Arthur done asked me to bring you all some madeira this morning," she said, holding up a green bottle of wine.

"No!" they all said in unison.

The black woman grinned, a gap in the front revealing several missing teeth. "Too early in the day, huh?"

Rob suddenly wondered if the head cook had a hand in doctoring the wine. "Did you add something to the Madeira last night?" he asked.

Annabelle just grinned back at him. "Mr. Arthur done tells me 'xactly how he wants his wine and food. Ain't up to me to make them decisions."

"Have you seen my sister?" Jason abruptly asked, changing the subject.

"Can't say I have. Not since last night. I put out the beef like she asked. It's gone this mornin', so she's 'bout someplace. Never seen such an appetite."

"Not like you folks." She lifted the top of a silver-plated server and frowned, looking inside. "All those nice sausages gone to waste."

What was the woman talking about? Rob walked over, looked inside the server, and gagged. Once fat sausages crawled with grubs.

White-headed maggots.

For a second, he was back under an oak tree on the field at Gettysburg, trying to save his friend's life. Blood oozed from a hole in Jack's abdomen; on the edges of the wound, bottle fly maggots ate the putrid flesh. Too late. He was too late. He was always too late.

"Get this out of here!" he roared. "What kind of cook are you? I was going to ask for toast, but I'll make it myself."

The kitchen was filthy when he entered, pots unwashed, piled high on stovetops. Dark brown grease dripped onto the floor in the corner where the rack used to roast sides of beef had been left untouched.

Uncleaned.

Flies marched up and down the length of the metal rods, and he shivered. He hated flies. Hated maggots even more.

Jo came up to his side. "Rob, this house is deteriorating quickly. Are you sure we can't leave?"

"We might have to leave just to eat. Maybe the Glen House after all, though I am loathe to bring danger once more to their doors."

He found an uncut loaf of bread in one of the kitchen drawers and quickly sliced several pieces, which Jo buttered. She gathered up an unopened jar of jam, and they brought everything back to the dining room. So much for toast. Isobel and Jason huddled in the corner, whispering as they watched Annabelle slamming the silver-plated servers onto a cart, muttering the entire time, "No damned Niggers in this house. We all be free."

Rob listened to the litany of words, over and over like a mantra. "That's right, Annabelle. You are free. You are free to go where you like."

"Masta no like such talk."

"There is no masta any more, Annabelle. You are a free woman."

"Mr. Arthur be the masta now."

"No, you are wrong. Arthur would never condone keeping anyone as a slave."

The black woman burst out in laughter, tears running down her face. "You don't understand. There always been a masta in *this* house."

She walked away shaking her head, pushing the cart in front. As she reached the doorway, she stopped and turned toward them. "Mr. Arthur says you go meet him at the carriage house." A sly little smile flitted across her lips. "You hurry now," she said, then left.

Rob sat for a minute, spreading strawberry jam as he considered Annabelle's words. "Jason, how long has Annabelle worked for your father?"

"Since I was a baby, at least that's what I've been told. My mother was a southerner and died in childbirth, same as Alison's mother two years earlier. Annabelle and Alice pretty much raised us. Neither of us knew our mothers. That was before the war, when you met him."

"And you've always lived here?"

"Yes, my whole life."

Rob knew the birthing process was dangerous, but could Jason's account be that coincidental? That both women died giving birth within a couple of years of each other? Anyway, they had more serious things to consider at the moment.

The large room grew quiet as they munched on slices of bread and jam.

Jason rose, emitting a slight belch. "My apologies. Gas from last night. Let me go out back and see if the Freed boys have dropped off any milk. They usually come by daily. Some milk will ease my stomach."

Within minutes, he was back with a wire rack holding two bottles of milk, cream rising at the top.

"Oh, that looks good." Isobel quickly found glasses inside one of the sideboards, and Jason poured them each a glass of milk, quickly downing his own. Isobel giggled when he looked at her, for his upper lip wore a ring of cream.

"Too bad I'm not a cat," she said, then blushed as she realized where they were.

"Moving right along, I'd like to institute several new rules," Rob said, ignoring her exchange. "Number One, no one, and that includes me, is ever to be alone from now on. No one, nowhere, including the chamber pot. Someone is to be on the other side of the screen at all times. Understood? This creature is fast. I don't think it can come inside the house. At least, not yet. But I don't want to take any chances. If you go fetch a bottle of milk, someone goes with you. Understood?"

He glanced at Jason, and the younger man nodded.

"Number Two: No more drinking wine of any sort. Jo had a very strange reaction to the madeira last night, and I'm pretty sure the bottle was contaminated with something beforehand."

A dark red flush climbed up Isobel's neck, rising to her earlobes and confirming Rob's suspicions. He would need to meet with Jason in private later and supply the young man with a source of condoms.

"Number Three." He took a deep breath. This one would be tough. "We are all going to sleep in one room from now on. At least until we figure out exactly what is going on. I propose our suite, as it is the largest. Women in the bed; Jason and I can sleep on the sofas from the antechamber. We'll pull them into the bedroom tonight."

"Any questions?" He looked around the room and realized they all stared at him, sort of slack-jawed. "All right, let's go find Arthur."

CHAPTER TWELVE

A large cardboard sign on the carriage house door said "GO AWAY."

"Now what?" Jason glared at the door, then whirled around, arms across his chest. "My father is an asshole. There, I've said it. I can't stand the man."

"Get a hold, Jason. We don't even know who wrote that sign."

The younger man glanced at Rob, hesitated for a minute, then nodded. Ever since the old gypsy woman told him he wasn't Arthur's son, he'd been roiling for a fight, a confrontation with the old man. With almost anyone, actually!

Everyone but Isobel.

"You are not begotten by the one you call father. It is a lie." The old crone had said something like that. He probably should have written the words down. Asked her how she knew such a thing. He'd felt so devastated at the time…still was; he hadn't had the presence of mind to ask her anything.

He had just wanted to get out of that damn tent.

And how could he know if what the old crone had told him was true? How would she know?

How *could* she know?

He should have told his friends the truth earlier in the dining room when Rob asked him about his mother.

Instead, he hadn't told anyone what the gypsy had said, not even Isobel, who at the moment gazed up at him with adolescent admiration. In the light of day, he felt disgusted that he'd touched her last night. They hadn't consummated the act, but had come damned close.

Christ! What was wrong with him? When he'd first met Isobel, he'd thought her a child still, maybe thirteen. Beautiful, but a child. Then he'd learned she was almost an adult. At seventeen, many girls were married with a child on the way. But Isobel and her older sister had suffered many setbacks growing up. Apparently, Isobel's psychological growth had been stunted, which is why Dr. Radnor was both her brother-in-law and her doctor.

What had he been thinking to invite her into his room? Not that she had argued. She had suggested it.

But he was the adult. The man in control. Except he'd had little to no control last night.

He felt the heat rise in his cheeks as he pictured Isobel throwing herself onto his bed. She had been shoeless. When had she lost her shoes? And she hiked up her skirts and looked at him with the most devastating expression.

Dark. Sultry.

Sort of like she had silently asked, "What's keeping you?"

How was a fellow supposed to act with an invitation like that?

Except as soon as he had started kissing her, he regained something of his senses. This was Isobel. He really liked her. But he had stroked her small breast a little, and as soon as she'd started to moan, he couldn't stop his hand from venturing under her skirts.

Oh, God. He could still feel the sensation of her slick nether lips beneath his fingertips.

When she began to thrash about, holding onto his neck like a log in a raging flood, pulling him down on top of her, he'd become scared. He could admit it now. Plain scared.

He'd literally jumped from the bed and tucked his shirt back into his trousers. "That's enough, Imp," he said, the words strangled in his throat. When had he started calling her Imp? Just like Dr. Radnor? Sort of a pet name. Like a pet.

Only Isobel was no pet. She had smiled at him, the same sultry sort of little grin, but her pearly white teeth looked sharp enough to rip his throat out.

"Whatever you want, Jason," she had replied, but he knew she taunted him, so he swiftly sat down in the oak Windsor chair in the corner of the room and crossed his legs. He felt he needed some sort of protection, which was ridiculous.

He was a grown man at least six feet tall.

His control apparently brought Isobel to her senses, for she tucked her legs beneath her petticoats and sighed, while the sharpness of her features softened. Perhaps her appearance had been entirely a figment of his imagination earlier. What he had wanted to happen. Not the reality of what truly happened.

Perhaps he had entirely made up parts of her behavior? What was truth and what was fantasy?

He no longer knew.

They'd begun to talk at that point, and Isobel shared her early life remembrances with him; growing up on a Midwest farm out in the middle of nowhere. She'd been a baby when her father sent them away, so she had no memory of him, nor the farmers and their wives coming to the orphan train to bid on them. She appeared to have very little memory of anything until around the age of seven, when one of the farmhands began bribing her sister Jo. Have sex with him - or he would initiate her younger sister.

The two girls apparently conspired to come up with a plan to stop the field hand they called Sly. Isobel went into one of the silos and climbed up, sliding out one of the grain chutes and fell to the ground, unconscious and later, unable to walk. The farm owners, afraid they would lose Jo, their best hay baler, saw that Isobel remained confined to her bed, and Sly was put under watch to keep him away from the two girls. Only Jo was no longer a girl. In her late teens by then, Sly tormented her constantly, egged on by the other farmhands.

One night the girls received a solicitor's letter, delivered to their room by the farmer's wife. They learned their father had died and left them a fortune. Isobel had no memory of the man, but her sister held only hatred for the bastard who sent them away on an orphan train, instead of acting like a father should.

Later that night, Jo was accosted by Sly and realized he had been watching them both through a peephole in their bedroom wall. When he returned to the girls' bedroom to rape Jo, she killed him by accident when the bedroom caught on fire.

Jason listened quietly for hours as Isobel shared her convoluted tale, amazed that either sister remained sane after such an incredibly difficult childhood.

He had gone to his balcony window to catch some air when he noticed his sister standing naked on the front lawn. The almost full moon highlighted her tall form and her long dark hair, which she appeared to be ripping from her head and throwing to the ground.

His sister had always been odd, and as a child, he often wondered if they were really related. But in his wildest daydreams, he never pictured her as she had been last night—totally deranged, insane, and crazy as she ran into the woods.

"So Jason, if you believe there is a cave up on that ridge, we probably need some torches. What else?"

Rob's question brought him back to the present.

"Some of the arrows," he suggested, feeling more than a little awkward. Rob kept looking at him with the oddest expression. He was pretty sure the older man knew exactly what Isobel and he had been doing last night. God, what a mess.

"But you have no bow," Isobel argued. "What good would they be?"

"Who knows," Rob agreed, "but I'd like some sort of weapon, and I rather doubt a gun will work. I'll bring Boromar, of course, but I don't know what sort of power he'll have over a Wendigo, if any at all."

The entire conversation sounded so ordinary, yet everything they discussed was as far from normal as possible. Jason looked at the three people standing across from him, and strangely, his heart gave a little pitter-patter of joy.

Once complete strangers, these three were the closest thing to a real family he had ever known. And he would be damned if anything would hurt them.

CHAPTER THIRTEEN

I t took less than an hour to gather the items they thought might be needed: ropes, torches, wax-covered matches, canteens of water, knives, and, upon his urging, one of Jason's rifles, though Rob seriously doubted Jason's weapon would stop the Wendigo. On his back, Rob bore the ancient quiver full of silver-tipped arrows. Without a bow, what good they would do he couldn't fathom, but he felt better for carrying them.

In his left hand, he gripped Boromar.

Until now, they had only seen the Wendigo's lair from across the lake. Climbing the steep cliff to gain access to the cave proved to be quite a challenge. The two women, once again dressed in men's trousers, lagged behind, initially holding hands until everyone resorted to scrambling on hands and knees up one particularly overgrown section of sharp, rock-strewn cliff face.

They were all out of breath by the time they reached the top. Rob called for a well-deserved break, and they quietly ate a couple of oatmeal cookies and drank some water. No one spoke; they knew what they needed to do. Still, Jo nervously glanced around the entire time she drank from her canteen. Rob smiled, hoping to reassure the woman he loved and send some color back into her cheeks.

Nothing helped.

She held her forefinger to her lips and motioned for him to come near. "I think the cave is around that bend up ahead," she whispered. "I can smell the creature."

Indeed, from where she stood, there was an odd odor on the breeze—something he couldn't quite place. Perhaps the moist, damp smell of her sweat mingled with the sweet, sickly odor of death. He nodded, then motioned to Isobel and Jason, mouthing the word "CLOSE."

Single file, the two couples slowly walked along the narrow path and rounded the corner. There, a huge, dark, yawning hole opened into the rock wall, partially covered by dead vines hanging from above. Nothing grew around the entry, just tangled brown grasses, trodden into the earth. The odor was so strong now, sickly sweet, a mixture of rotted flesh and worse.

Jo forced back the sour bile in her mouth, swallowing repeatedly until she was sure her stomach was under control. Rob's face gleamed white from stress; sweat glistened on his brow. She had never seen him this afraid. She wanted to turn around and run, but knew that wasn't the solution. From deep inside the cave, the faint murmur of a woman's wailing drifted on the breeze.

They needed to go in.

Taking one last deep breath, Jo entered the cave right behind Rob. As he bent forward to peer into the inky blackness, one of his arrows caught on an overhead rock and fell before her. Without thinking, she scooped it up and immediately became aware of the warmth in her palm, as though the arrow recognized her touch. Odd!

Flickering light danced off the rocky ceiling as Jason lit a torch behind them, illuminating the depths of the immediate cavern. The cave wasn't as large as she had expected, tapering off rapidly to a dark tunnel entrance in the far wall. Isobel hung behind Jason, clutching his hand, her sister's eyes squeezed tight from fear. Maybe they should have left her behind, but in truth, none of them were safe anywhere.

Rob stepped into the tunnel entrance, Jo right behind him. A faint breeze wafted around her, surrounded by the rotting, sweet stench of death. She gagged but determinedly stepped one foot in front of the other. The moving air indicated there had to be another entry point somewhere up ahead.

As they slowly walked down the tunnel, the sound of what she believed was a woman keening became louder, interspersed with a mumble of laughter, then the words, "Yummy. Yummy. So good to eat."

Alison's voice.

Dread filled Jo's heart. Had Alison actually been the Wendigo all along?

Rob's steps slowed even more. Darkness gave way to faint gray as they entered a much larger cave.

They walked in together and stopped. Sitting on the rock floor in the far corner, a dark, formless creature stared up at them, eyes flashing, dried red blood congealed around the lipless hole that once had been its mouth. A long thigh bone dangled from taloned feet as it continued to pick small bits of meat from the bone and stuff them into the gaping hole.

"Umm. So hungry," it mumbled, then gave out a high-pitched keen, a laugh like no other.

Alison, naked, stark raving mad.

A moan sounded behind them. Jason.

"Sister. Come from here," he whispered. The creature hissed as its woman's body shape took form and slowly rose to its feet.

The woman appeared much taller than Jo remembered, and even thinner, if possible. The top of her head was bald, while what was left of her once luxurious black hair now hung in scraggly threads about her emaciated face. She dropped the large bone from her taloned fingers, and as it fell, a sparkling gold ring tinkled on the rock floor.

Arthur's emerald.

Alison had consumed her father.

"So hungry," she said, and took a step towards Rob, who appeared frozen with fear.

"Rob, don't let her get close," Jo said clearly.

The creature took another step closer, then another.

"Rob!" she screamed when he didn't move.

Slowly, Rob raised his left fist, the wolf-headed cane snarling and twisting before him.

In that instant, the arrow in Jo's palm burned red hot, searing her skin. The creature was almost upon Rob. Two steps more, and it would be too late.

Jo threw herself forward, arrow upraised. Unable to stab Alison in the eye, the arrow pierced her breast as Jo thrust it deep into the creature's chest. Alison fell backwards, Jo on top.

"Oh, God!" she screamed as the slimy feel of Alison's naked skin peeled off beneath her hands. Melting flesh bubbled on the rock floor as Alison began to dissolve beneath her.

Jo scrambled to her feet and ran to Rob's side. Across from them, Jason sobbed into Isobel's hair.

Within seconds, only bits of Alison's body remained, quickly congealing into a black rock. In the center, one red eye stared up at them.

"Aarrgh!" sounded from deep on the other side of the large cavern.

A monstrous, whirling black animal entered.

The Wendigo was fast upon them.

CHAPTER FOURTEEN

The sickening stench of the gray miasma that enveloped them was too strong to fight. Isobel slumped to her knees, then rolled into a ball on the floor of the cave. Jason huddled on top as though for protection.

Rob leaned on Boromar, though the cane rendered little support. Jo alone remained on her feet, staring back into the Wendigo's eerie yellow eyes as it peered down at her.

"You brought the Hunter with you," Jo heard it say, though the creature had no lips—just a gaping black hole where silver drool hung down. Could the fiend be referring to Rob, who struggled to stand upright?

The creature stared at the silver ring on Jo's pinkie finger, then growled.

"You have taken the one I loved above all others, even myself."

The Wendigo bent down and picked up what was left of Alison, cuddling the black rock in the crook of its arm. Jo noticed the line of hair running up the Wendigo's backbone, like a ridge of fur on a brown dog's back. Outside of her control, her arm reached up to stroke the creature, her fingertips tingling hot, then burning the closer she got.

She watched Rob straighten up and reach over his shoulder, drawing forth one of the silver-tipped arrows.

The Wendigo snarled, and a massive blue tongue ran around the outside of the lipless chasm that served as its mouth. "Not so fast, Hunter," it growled. "We will meet again."

In a flash and swirl of light, the enormous creature disappeared down the dark tunnel.

An eerie quiet descended on the cave.

"Well, that was fun," Jason remarked drily, helping Isobel to her feet.

"I thought it would kill you," she whispered, staring hard at Jo. "Why didn't it? And why did you try to touch it?"

"I don't know," Jo heard herself say. "I felt sorry for it. So alone."

Rob reached her side and gathered her close. "Well, I have an idea it might just want a replacement for Alison in the future."

Jo shuddered in his arms. "Please kill me before I reach that stage. Please!"

"I think you're wrong," Isobel whispered, pointing to the far back of the cave. The flicker of Jason's torch bounced off the stark white of a giant skull resting on the cave floor.

"So the Wendigo robbed that grave." Rob grimaced as he rolled the head over with the toe of his boot. "Perhaps it ate some of the dead body." Two vacant eye sockets stared up at him. At some point, someone or something had laced the skull's jawbone to the upper palate using thick black string. Rob knelt down on one knee and peered at the threading. He realized the jawbone was actually inscribed with Anasazi symbols: a stick figure dog. Could that represent the Wendigo? The crescent moon, a flower bud—others he didn't recognize. Except in the middle of them all was a large triangle. A black DOT represented each triangle point, and in the middle of the triangle, another larger DOT—the ancient Anasazi symbol of protection from beasts and phantoms.

Had the Wendigo brought the skull to the cave? Or had it been left as a warning to the creature by others, years ago?

"More Anasazi writing. This is getting a little redundant," Rob said sarcastically. "It would be helpful if I could read them all."

"Should we bring the skull with us?" Jo whispered. Coming to his side, she knelt down as well. "If it belongs to the Indian, perhaps we should return it to his grave."

"I was wondering the same thing," Rob replied, taking her hand, which felt unusually warm and sweaty. "But it seems to have been left here as a talisman of some sort."

"Well, it didn't bring *us* much protection," Jo said sharply, standing upright and pulling Rob to his feet. "We need to leave this place and not return."

CHAPTER FIFTEEN

As it turned out, the trip down the cliffside took much longer to navigate than the climb up. All the way down, Jason pondered the gypsy hag's words. Since the day of the fair, he had told no one, trying to unravel the mystery. If she told the truth, then Arthur wasn't his father. If she hadn't told the truth, the seeds of doubt had been sown. Either way, why had she told him such a thing? And how could she have known?

When the path finally flattened, he stopped walking.

"It is time I confess," he said. The others stood there blankly, just staring at him.

"What in the world would you have to confess to?" Isobel said softly. She reached out and squeezed his hand, and the tension in his shoulders released.

Thank God for good friends.

He cleared his throat, but couldn't find the words he looked for. "Well, first of all, I didn't add anything to the wine. That has to have been my father's doing. Only Arthur's not really my father. And as for those footsteps on your bedroom floor, maybe that was the ghost my sister said haunted Miramar Hall. And as for..."

Isobel took a step away from him. "What on earth are you rambling on about?"

Rob took a step toward him, his features narrowing. "Yes, Jason. What are you rambling on about? Your circumlocution is getting us nowhere."

Jason's features squinched up as he fought back tears. "Oh, fuck it!" he yelled. "According to the gypsy woman, Arthur is not my father."

Rob took another step toward him, lips taut, almost white from tension. "I thought that was what you said. What sort of foolishness is this?"

"You remember. The day of the fair, when we all ended up at the gypsy camp. Before Isobel and Jo went into the fortune-telling tent, the old woman drew me inside and said something like the man you call father did not beget you. Something like that. I should have written it down."

Isobel reached out and squeezed his hand then, hard. Maybe in reassurance? Or was she as afraid as he felt? "I knew she told you something that day from the way you looked—so dejected, so sad. Why would she tell you something like that? I don't understand."

"I don't know," Jason agreed. "It's why I haven't said anything before now. It's been weighing on my mind. Why would Arthur pretend to be my father? Did he adopt me? Who was my real father?"

Rob's eyelids narrowed in frustration. "So many secrets and so little time." Sarcasm tinged his words. "I'm afraid Arthur was the only one who could have answered those questions, Jason. And I don't think he's still alive, do you?"

Jason hung his head. "I can't speak for the others, but that's the last of my secrets," he mumbled. He knew he should feel badly that Arthur was dead, but he felt nothing but anger toward the man.

He noticed Isobel and Jo frantically whispering back and forth, no doubt equally angry with him. Why hadn't he told them the truth from the beginning? What was the matter with him? Just like Alison always said, he was a complete failure at everything he tried.

From the corner of his eye, he caught a glimpse of something dark and immense, deep in the woods off to their right—a cloud-like form hidden among the white birch and dark green and brown pines. Jason quickly caught up to the women in front and hurried them along. His imagination had taken hold, no doubt, but he wasn't taking any chances.

Dusk drew nigh as they walked up the long driveway to Miramar Hall. The ancient stone walls thrust into the fading sunlight, appearing ominous against the darkening sky. The air felt heavy, the threat of a thunderstorm looming in the distance.

Normally, Rob enjoyed the approach of dusk. At the moment, though, his thoughts capriciously darted from one idea to another.

In a way, it was probably just as well that Arthur no longer lived. How could you tell a man his daughter had turned into a monstrous man-eater? Or that all she could have been was now reduced to an ever-staring, bright red eye, forever the property of a lovestruck demon?

As they drew near the main house, Rob's breath caught in his throat. A man sat in the shadows of the top step, feet splayed wide in front, head hung dejectedly low between two slouched shoulders. In his hands, he held a wide-brimmed hat.

"Arthur, we thought you were dead," Rob said, his words so quiet he wondered if the man heard them.

Then the man glanced up, and Jason said, "Not my father, Rob. Wiley. Why are you here, old man?"

The scrawny soldier stood up, slapping the hat against the front of his trousers.

"No place else to go now. They're all gone—dead or run off. Just the five of us left, I reckon."

The man glanced at the hat he held. "This be the cap'n's hat. He done went stark raving mad, ran into the woods looking for the demon. I heard his screamin' this afternoon and went to look. His body was torn to pieces, some parts missing, I might add."

Rob shuddered, recalling Alison's twisted features as she deftly picked meat off Arthur's thigh bone and stuffed it into the gaping hole she'd once called her mouth.

"You've been with the captain a long time, haven't you, Wiley?" Rob's words were soft but pointed. The elderly soldier stared at him hard, weighing his answer. "Guess no harm done now," he finally said, spitting in the grass. "The cap'n's gone; the masta's gone. Ain't no harm to be done, and better the truth be told."

"You, boy," he said, pointing a dirty-nailed finger in Jason's face. "You ain't no son of the cap'n. Neither one of you children come of his blood."

"Who then?" asked Jason, his face ashen, sweat dotting his brow.

"Why, the masta', of course."

Rob stepped forward, placing a firm hand on Jason's shoulder. "I think he means George Trenholm, treasurer of the Confederacy."

The old soldier nodded briskly. "That be right. Masta' Tren tried to do right by us all, even his slaves. He shipped his half-ens up to the cap'n to raise in exchange for all those trunks of gold we buried in the Indian grave."

"What do you mean, half-ens?" Jason's voice broke on the last word, his anguish evident.

"Why, son, half black, of course."

Jason took a step back and swayed, his forearm braced against his forehead as though hit with the force of a giant rock. "Oh my God."

Rob grabbed the younger man's shoulders with both hands. "Jason, this is not the end of the world," but Jason pulled away.

The old soldier wouldn't stop talking. "I recall the meetin' as clear as yesterday. I give you these two babies to raise as your own. Mulatto by birth, but as white-skinned as myself. Slaves no longer; I dare not keep them with me. The masta' was a right proud man, and he knew prison awaited, so he saved his two most prized children."

"Prized for what?" Jason said bitterly. "To be paraded around like cattle or horses? No wonder Arthur treated me with so little respect. And Alison, my dear half-sister, what about her?"

Wiley took a step back, cringing slightly from the force of Jason's words. "Her mother was one of Masta' Tren's house slaves, like your own."

"You mean BLACK, let's be clear!" Jason spat out. "And what did you mean, his two most prized children? You mean there are more of us?"

"No, no, young man. Your mother and Alison's were prized mulattos, light-skinned as any of us. They'd pass for white folk anywhere. Masta' Tren put great store in both your mothers. They was happy to see their children head north to grow up white. Slaves no longer."

Jason's jaw tightened as he grit his teeth in frustration. "It makes no difference, don't you see? My entire life is a lie."

"That's true, son. The cap'n took great pride in Miss Alison. There was more of a connection there than between father and daughter, if you know what I mean."

The old soldier winked slyly. Across from them, Rob fought hard for control, then gave up and knocked the man off his feet.

Jason started to laugh, despite his anguish. "Thanks, Rob. If you hadn't done that, I would have."

The old soldier rubbed his jaw, then scrambled to his feet. "There weren't no cause for you to do that," he spat out, glaring at Rob, then wiped the back of his grimy hand across his lips. "No cause a'tall. Masta' Tren was an honorable man. Someone this youngster should be proud to call father," he added, pointing directly at Jason.

"You wanted the truth, but you ain't man enough to accept it," he continued. "Your real father was a director of the Bank of Charleston and then became director of the Blue Ridge railroad. Fraser, Trenholm & Company served as the Confederate government's overseas banker. When he learned the Rebs was coming to arrest him, he sent you two young'uns to the cap'n. He saved you and your sister both. No tellin' what would have happened to you."

Jason laughed bitterly. "What you're really saying is Arthur accepted us into his house in exchange for Confederate gold. A lot of it! And now the gold is gone."

The old soldier slammed Arthur's hat on his head. "Well, I ain't giving none of mine back, if that's what you're suggestin'."

"I'm not suggesting anything. I'm telling you I want you out of here, now."

As they watched the old soldier shuffle down the driveway, Rob smiled, then shook Jason's hand. "Well done. As for Arthur's missing gold, I've a mind to go visit the gypsies, if you're all up for another adventure. I think it's time for us to learn the real truth."

Jason moaned but nodded in agreement. "Why not," he muttered, turning away. "I've nothing to keep me here."

CHAPTER SIXTEEN

As it turned out, they spent another night at Miramar Hall. A quiet night. Crammed into Rob and Jo's suite, the two couples spent hours discussing strategy. Rob and Jason recovered several reference books from Arthur's library, and towards the back of one of them, Rob discovered a short dictionary of Anasazi symbols written in Greek.

Next to the stick-like dog figure were the Greek letters **AVOPOoaYOI.** Literal Greek translation: man-eaters. According to Herodotus, this was another name for the Androphagi, the ancient nation of cannibals who dwelled in the dense forests north of Scythia.

Jo and Isobel sat in the middle of the bed, wide-eyed, as Rob read from the Greek text. "Years ago, I first came across mention of the Androphagi in writings by Pliny the Elder," he explained, glancing up from the ancient Greek dictionary. "I was researching an ancient water fern, Salvinia, and came across the word mard-xwaar in old Iranian, which literally can be translated as man-eater. I never actually believed those people existed. Figured it was more like another morality tale from the Bible."

A snort escaped from Isobel, and she began to giggle. "So you think our Wendigo is an Androp...whatever you called it? That sounds too bizarre to be true."

Rob reached over and ruffled Isobel's hair. "All I know for sure, Imp, is that there are many ancient references to man-eaters and cannibals. Here, let me read this from Pliny the Elder: *The Androphagi were in the habit of drinking from human skulls, and placing the scalps with the hair attached upon their own breasts to terrify their enemies.*"

Rob closed the book and placed it in his lap. "Yes, I think that would terrify me."

Jo shook her head. "What if instead of fastening the scalps to their chests, they wore them on their backs, like that ridge of fur on the Wendigo's back?"

Isobel stared at her sister. "So now *you* believe this Pliny guy?"

"I believe this is an ancient creature," Jo said, "perhaps not of this world. How it got here or where it came from isn't really important." She sighed and stretched out her legs. "I do know that people thousands of years ago talked about them and wrote about them, which convinces me they existed then, and they exist now."

Rob rose to his feet. "Let's get some sleep, and maybe one of us will come up with an idea on how to kill this ancient thing."

It was well after noon when they located the gypsy camp deep in the Moultonborough woods, spread out at the base of a large barren hill that jutted above the ancient pines. The land was curious. The hill itself appeared to have burned to the soil years earlier, but the dense forest surrounding its base remained untouched. Gypsy tents and wagons were scattered helter-skelter among the trees, with the old crone's hut hidden beneath the boughs of an ancient spruce that towered above the emerald forest.

Rob reined in front of her hut, and they all piled out, heading towards the doorway where a young man watched their approach. Jo suspected he was the same youth they'd seen digging at the Indian grave the day they arrived at Miramar Hall.

He went inside, and within seconds, the elderly crone emerged, leaning on a wooden cane.

"Now that you have come to believe," the old gypsy announced, "it is time for you to learn." As she spoke, the woods around them rustled, and from behind different tree trunks, children's faces appeared, pinched and drawn. The people living in this camp might work for food, but it appeared the pay was meager from the New Hampshire farmers.

The old woman settled onto a narrow wooden chair the young man had retrieved from inside the hut. The top of the chair back was adorned with an oak board engraved with a crescent moon above a trident lying on its side. The gypsy children settled on the ground to listen to the old woman's words as though she were recounting a Bible story of great importance.

"We gypsies have existed on these lands for many eons, driven from Europe out of fear and prejudice. What was called a Werewolf in Europe became a Wendigo here. The never-ending battle between good and evil. We gypsies never brought the evil here; we can only predict when it will appear and how to fight it."

"So how do we fight it?" Rob asked quietly, drawing closer, with Jo at his side. "Should we retrieve the skull?"

The elderly woman, who seemed to shrink in front of them, pointed one long finger at Jo. "You have learned what you needed to learn. It was sent to you for a reason."

Jo shook her head, the crone's cryptic words making little sense.

Rob approached the small front porch and went down on one knee. Jo stood right behind him. "Ancient Shiva queen Parvati, goddess of Mahadeva, I bring you a present."

He held out one of the silver-tipped arrows. She rose and accepted it, fingering the silver band holding the arrowhead in place.

"I am fighting something I don't understand," Rob said slowly. "Something that shouldn't exist in the real world."

"There are many worlds," the old woman replied, "and they all exist, sometimes crossing back and forth." She lifted her head and stared at Rob for a minute. "Anasazi," she whispered. "You alone can fight the Wendigo. While you all have the weapons, she must wield them, though."

She looked at Jo, her eyes dark and hard, then said slowly, "She does not know her true self, nor her purpose. But this is her test, and she alone can find the way. You will need this," she added, handing the arrow to Jo. Then she dropped her cane and seized Jo's chin with both hands, staring deep into her eyes. "Look through the door that has no key; accept the scroll of your prior life. Read the secret symbols of your earthbound strife; waste not God's lilies with feeble deeds."

Then she slumped back into her chair. "Now leave me. My time is short, and I must rest. My grandson will take you to the gold."

Rob shook his head. "We are not here for the gold, Parvati, but to hear your words of wisdom only, and to gain your help."

"Your time is short for what?" Jo asked, but the old crone refused to speak further. They finally gave up and left.

"May you go with our ancient blessings upon you," her grandson said gravely as he stepped off his grandmother's porch.

"And on you," Rob replied. But all he could think was, *We need more weapons.*

CHAPTER SEVENTEEN

He'd never thought himself capable of such thoughts. Yet, here he was.

Moreover, he knew his thoughts to be true. Jo was the only one who could save them now.

Rob glanced down at his wife's face, turned towards him in sleep. Dark red hair spilled across the pillows—a sea of red. Quiet and calm. Beautiful, but still. Steadfast. That was the word. More than anything, Jo was steadfast to the end. She had saved her sister years ago, and by doing so, had saved herself. Perhaps the old crone was right. Perhaps Jo could save them all this time.

⁂

Jo sensed, more than felt, Rob slip out of their bed.

Their bed.

Though Rob's initial plan had been for the women to sleep together in the bed and the men on individual chaises, the plans quickly changed once they'd actually retired.

The cool night air rushed into the empty space where he'd slept, then just as quickly, Rob pulled the covers back over her. She remained quiet, knowing he was on the prowl—restless as always once they'd confirmed the Wendigo's existence.

Truth be told, she didn't dare move, too afraid to follow him.

Long after he'd gone, Jo lay there listening to the timid thud of her faithless heart.

Across the room, Isobel thrashed in her sheets until Jason pulled them up under her chin, then rolled over and began to snore lightly.

"I am so sorry, Rob," Jo whispered into the night, knowing in her soul she'd always been a coward. She'd spent years arguing otherwise, but the truth was, she'd always run away, and probably always would.

In the morning, Rob explained his thoughts over breakfast: the last loaf of bread and a jar of blackberry jam. Isobel stared at him with pink-rimmed eyes. "You want my sister to do what?" she sputtered. "This is the most insane thing you've ever proposed."

Jason stood up beside her. "That does sound a little desperate, Rob. Jo is a small woman, slightly built. How could she possibly kill a demon?"

Rob shook his head in frustration. "Not kill it, just lure it into the house. Last night, while you all slept, I started inscribing an Anasazi protective circle on the den floor. Once finished, if the Wendigo steps inside it, he won't be able to leave."

"You told me days ago the monster couldn't enter the house," Jo whispered, her back turned. When she whirled to face them, tears welled in the corners of her eyes. "Were you lying then, or lying now?"

Rob's head began to throb. "Jo... Josie, I have never lied to you."

Jo's foot tapped repetitively on the floor. "That's a lie right there!" she exclaimed. "That summer at the Glen House, you tricked my sister and me more times than I can count. Speaking of which, yesterday you said maybe we should go on to the Glen House? What has changed your mind? And shouldn't the rest of us have something to say about the decision?"

"Why are you bringing up what happened five years ago?" Rob countered, anger tinging his words. "It serves no purpose now. I did what I had to. I was trying to save you both."

"No purpose to you, perhaps," Isobel interjected. "But this is Jo's life you're playing with." She went to her sister's side and put an arm around her shoulders. Jo clenched her sister's waist.

"I will take her place," Isobel announced bravely.

Jo slumped into her sister's side. "Hush. Rob is right; no one can do it but me. We all heard the gypsy crone."

A headache lurked behind Rob's eyes, and he squinted in the morning light. The ebony head of his ivory cane warmed beneath his thumb, and his fist tightened. He couldn't give in to his fears. This had to work. They had no other choice.

"There are many worse things that can happen than death," he ground out.

Jo remembered Alison congealing into a black rock; the feel of the woman's body melting into the cave floor beneath her. She shivered as early morning sunlight beamed into the sitting room. Would she ever feel warm again?

"I'll try," she said softly, "but how?"

Rob nervously cleared his throat. "We've all seen the creature outside of the cave. I saw it dancing on the veranda in the moonlight with Alison just a few days ago. So it has been just outside this house. What if I bring you up to the cave this afternoon, Jo? Not to go inside. But you could call to it, invite it to join you tonight."

Isobel's cheeks grew bright red with anger. "Oh, God. That is gross, Rob. Jo can't do that. No one could. How could you ask such a thing?"

Rob whirled on them, breathless with anger. "I would never allow that beast to touch her!" he gasped. "This is simply a ploy, a trick to get the creature to step inside the circle. Then I will kill it with one of the Anasazi arrows. Hopefully, the circle will be strong enough to hold it until we can cut off its head."

An involuntary shudder rolled over his chest. "I would never want Jo to be within ten feet of that thing again. Not ever."

⚜

The Anasazi circle danced beneath their feet, stark white with chalk embedded into the lines and symbols Rob had carved into the dark oak floor. Jo had no idea what the symbols meant as she peered down at the stick-limbed drawings. Intricately detailed, she prayed the awkward figures held the power to capture the Wendigo.

"Will it work?" she whispered.

Rob's arms surrounded her from behind, his chin coming to rest on the top of her head. In a different time and place, such a move would have led to seduction. Now it only meant to comfort.

Jo sighed, wondering if they would ever make love again. *Will I even survive the night?*

She recalled the gypsy crone's words: *waste not God's lilies with feeble deeds.*

She sighed and leaned back into Rob's strength. This would be their moment; they would only get one.

Rob's arms tightened, as though sensing her quiet unease. "We will come through this," he whispered into her hair, reading her thoughts. "You are my strength, my life. I will not let the creature take you," he promised.

Jo felt the tightness between her shoulder blades flow away as he spoke, and she allowed herself to relax for the briefest of seconds.

The clasp of the door to the den grated as Jason led Isobel into the room. "We knew you lovebirds would be here," the young woman exclaimed. They drew apart as she approached. Jo watched Isobel closely, looking for signs or a signal. Her sister had been acting strangely for the past few days—one minute in tears, the next laughing like a hyena. They were all under the greatest of strains.

Isobel pointed towards their feet. "Rob, you've been in here working for hours. You need to explain what all these symbols mean. And how they will work."

Rob sighed but began to patiently explain what he'd carved into the floor. He'd learned long ago Imp never let up unless he answered all her questions.

Shutting out her sister's persistent chatter, Jo drew close to the front window. It had begun to rain, she noted, a quiet patter dancing across the veranda. Far off in the dense woods beyond, she watched a dark shape swirl beneath the canopy of pines and firs, then coalesce less than thirty yards away. The Wendigo needed no invitation but had arrived of its own volition.

Jo drew back from the window, hand at her mouth. "He has come for me," she whispered.

Hours later, they still sat in a huddle by the back door to the kitchen. The conversation flowed from fighting the monster to fleeing the monster. There was no consensus.

"You thought Jo would need to lure it here, but it has come on its own. Why do you think it is here?"

Isobel's question hung in the air. They'd all been asking themselves the same thing since the creature arrived, though the answer was quite obvious: it had come for Jo.

"Are you sure the protection circle is complete? What if you've forgotten something?" Jo said quietly. "What if it doesn't work?"

Jason began to pace the kitchen floor. "I think we should run. Jo and Rob should go first," he added. "Isobel and I will follow and try to distract the creature. If we can make it to the stables and the horses, we could simply ride out of here."

Rob sighed, running his fingertips over his grizzled chin. "We can't outrun the Wendigo," he said wearily. "My plan has to work." He picked up one of the silver-tipped arrows, turning it over in his palm, then offered it to Jo.

"This is the arrow the gypsy woman said was for you. You should keep it close now, for protection."

"I'm going outside," Jo said softly, rising to her feet. "I need to go now, before my courage runs out."

She rubbed the silver ring on her pinkie finger, praying Rob's Anasazi protection circle worked better than the talisman he had made for her. She looked at the arrow Rob proffered, then shook her head. "In a few hours, it will be dark. I don't think the Wendigo will wait. But we can't be sure. I don't want to be trapped in the den in the dark with that creature. It's better to see it in the light, where we can decide what to do. But if we can see the Wendigo, it can see us, and surely an arrow in my hand will reveal our trap."

Rob stared at her bleakly. "Do what you must do," he muttered hoarsely, gripping the arrow in his fist as he walked out of the kitchen. Jo hurried after him, but he strode down the long mahogany hallway and turned into the den, sliding the door shut behind him.

So much for sharing.

As she stepped outside, evening dusk swirled around her legs, the sun fading as though in an eclipse. Crickets cheerily greeted her, then fell silent. She walked down the front steps and stopped, her limbs frozen in time, unable to move.

"I see you have come to me at last." The Wendigo's whisper echoed in her head, though nothing emanated from the gaping black hole that once served as its mouth. The creature appeared much taller and broader than she remembered. How could they possibly destroy such a thing?

"No, I am here just to ask you to leave."

No one had suggested what she should say to the creature. Perhaps it was better to just speak the truth.

In a whirl, the creature was at her side. "That cannot be," it whispered in her head, its lipless mouth never moving. "From the moment I first saw you, I knew you were the one."

"The one what?"

"The one that will make me complete."

Jo noticed that under one skeletal-like arm, the Wendigo carried the enormous skull they'd first seen at the Wendigo's cave. Clearly, it held some significance for the creature.

He watched her eyes while he sniffed the air like a dog. "This was my brother once," he explained. "When we were young, we hunted the Wendigo's trail all the way across Canada, then down across the border. My brother ended up in that grave you found. I kept his head and went on. He should not have trusted the people who lived here; they killed him, believing him a Wendigo, when in truth it was I they hunted.

Jo shuddered as the creature began to laugh, the shape of its mouth never changing.

"Surely you didn't want to see him dead?" she asked. "You've kept his skull all this time."

"Ha! So pure and innocent you are. I always hated my brother! He was so proud, so God-like. He believed himself to be a great hunter. You see these symbols? I drew them for protection on his skull. Protection for ME. My brother walks this earth just like I do, only his is the walk of death, never to escape this earthbound hell. While my walk is one of enlightenment. Every day I grow stronger. The more I eat, the more I understand. Soon there will be no one, nothing that can stop me from my pleasures."

The Wendigo leaned forward and blew softly on her neck; bitter cold seeped into Jo's shoulder. "Soon you will come to know of what I speak."

In his free hand, he held up Alison, or rather the red-eyed stone she'd become. "This one was faithless to the end. She would not learn but simply gorged on the flesh that should have been mine. I am glad the glutton is gone."

Just like that, the Wendigo threw the stone across the yard, where it shattered into a thousand pieces, tiny black shards left to glitter in the fading sunlight.

"Let us go," the creature urged, trying to draw her ever closer to its side.

"I need to fetch some of my things. Come inside," she urged as the Wendigo drew back, its blue tongue tip darting this way and that. "I will go with you, but I want some of my clothes. I will not run naked like Alison."

"Yes, yes," the creature almost purred. He lowered his brother's skull to the grass. "I will help you. I thought about it all night. The other one grew crazy, unstable. You are the one I truly desire. We will become as one, knowing each other's mind as well as our own. You will be the purity I've always sought."

Jo doubted that but nodded in agreement. Anything to lure the Wendigo inside. As they crossed the threshold, all she could do was pray the others were ready.

CHAPTER EIGHTEEN

Rob stood just outside the Anasazi circle, his back to the room as he stared into the blazing fireplace. He heard the click of the metal hinge as the door to the den swung open; held his breath for a few seconds, the stench of the Wendigo's putrid, rotting flesh overwhelming as it entered the den.

"Why are you here?" the creature growled.

Rob turned to face him. "This is where we will make our sacred vows. This woman and I."

Rob pointed to Jo, who stood with her back pressed to the door, hand at her mouth. "She is mine. You cannot have her." He lifted Boromar in front of his chest; the black ebony wolf's head snarled, white fangs snapping.

A great roar emitted from the depths of the Wendigo's chest, the fireplace flames flickering before its force. Advancing on Rob, the demon creature grew larger by the second. Immense, fury black as hell. The blue tongue circled the outline of its lipless mouth, darting here and there, scenting Rob's blood in the air, anxious to drink its fill.

Rob took one step towards the creature, then another—just enough to bring himself inside the Anasazi circle. The creature hesitated, its head lolling back and forth as though contemplating any danger Rob might present.

Seeing none, it silently lunged forward.

Jo's scream pierced the room as the creature seized Rob by the throat, lifting him high above the floor. The Anasazi arrow Rob held behind his back clattered at their feet, and he dropped Boromar as he struggled to grab the top of the Wendigo's head. He felt the nubby skin peel away from the creature's skull like the carapace of a turtle.

Truly, the Wendigo was rotting away before their eyes.

The undead monstrosity shook his head violently, but Rob held on. Blood throbbed thick and heavy as the monster's grip tightened around his neck. His mind swirled, grew black.

Seconds, just seconds, or it'll be too late. I'll be gone... But the strength in his arms disappeared, and they fell limp to his sides.

The bony fingers digging into his neck loosened ever so slightly. Rob managed to glance down and saw a tip of silver protruding from the black sheen of skin covering the creature's chest. Jo had stabbed the Wendigo from behind with the Anasazi arrow.

With a howl of anger, the creature dropped Rob and fell to its knees, skeletal arms flailing behind its back as it attempted to locate the arrow. A soundless gasp rose from the gaping mouth. Then it fell forward, hunched over, palms on the hardwood floor, panting like a dog. Rob stumbled back against the fireplace, then looked down and saw the iron poker leaning against the bricks. With almost superhuman strength, he swung it high and brought the poker's sharp point crashing down on the Wendigo's skull.

A keening, high-pitched wail careened against the ceiling and walls as the creature crumpled to the floor. From the top of the crack on its head, grey fluid oozed, then began to flow quickly, puddling on the floor.

Could that be the Wendigo's blood? Or what remained of its brain?

The odor of rotten eggs filled the room, and Rob gagged, then saw Jo from the corner of his eye. She huddled against the far wall, face ashen, one arm and hand bent at an odd angle.

"Rob," she cried out to him, silent, but in his mind, and the warmth of her love embraced them both. Somehow, she was in his head, and he in hers.

"We must burn the creature, or the spirit of the Wendigo will prevail and return stronger than before," he whispered. "The Anasazi circle will only hold him so long."

She nodded, and he felt the fear and hesitation of her mind flee, as something much stronger took hold. Belief: belief in him, in his strength of purpose.

Most of all, belief in herself.

"As you wish, my love. Let's burn this cursed house to the ground." Her silent words were all Rob needed. One look at her crooked arm, and he knew it was broken, sensed the pain she kept at bay. Somehow, driving the Anasazi arrow into the Wendigo's back had caused her arm to buckle and collapse, her fingers curled uselessly in her palm.

Rob realized he still held the fireplace poker in his right fist. He drew near the raging fireplace and began to drag the burning logs out onto the floor, slowly encircling the white Anasazi symbols surrounding the Wendigo. The pyre soon grew into a wall of fire, and Jo pulled him from behind.

"We must run," she whispered in his head.

As they drew near the study door, a great roar once again enveloped the room. The Wendigo slowly crawled back to his feet, red eyes gleaming with hatred.

From the hallway outside, Jo heard Isobel call her name, then Jason began beating on the study door with his fists.

"It won't open," she heard the younger man call out as she glanced back at Rob. The room was quickly filling with smoke.

"The windows," she whispered, then louder. "Break a window."

Rob gripped the iron poker and drew Jo close to his chest, then pushed her behind him as he staggered towards the closest window, then swung the poker with all his might.

The panes of glass shattered outward, and a rush of cool air engulfed them, feeding the fire behind their backs.

"Do not leave me to burn. Anything but the fire. No, No!" the creature shrieked in pain, as the fire began to consume his melting flesh.

"Don't look back," Rob ordered as the two of them stumbled out of the broken window frame.

"No..o..o! No..o!" the Wendigo screamed again, slower this time, and Jo couldn't help but feel sorry for him; she felt the faint pull of the creature's mind trying to get her to return inside.

"Don't even consider it," Rob said roughly. He seized her chin and kissed her hard.

All concerns for the creature evaporated. What had she been thinking? Rob had almost died at the Wendigo's hands. Jo reached up and cupped the side of his face with her good fingers, feeling the stubble beneath her fingertips. They all needed a bath!

They ran around the side of the house; saw Isobel and Jason fleeing from the front door, flames reaching high behind them. Somewhere deep inside the bowels of the house, Jo could have sworn she heard the Wendigo calling to her, its voice much fainter now. When the flames finally cooled, she knew he would be completely gone, consumed by the fires of Hell.

CHAPTER NINETEEN

As red spilled off the edges of the earth and turned to black, the foursome slowly walked away from Miramar Hall. In just a few hours, what was left of the building seemed to crumble, then shrink into the ground. Where flowering bushes once graced the outside verandas, dead vines and brown twigs hung vacant and unadorned. The earth was reclaiming its own.

Under one arm, Rob carried the enormous Indian skull they had retrieved from the front lawn, where the Wendigo had placed it hours earlier. Each led a mount away from the smoldering embers that remained of Miramar Hall. Even the carriage house had burned in the inferno. By sheer willpower, they had managed to force their way inside the stable and free the horses. But hours passed before they could find a few that didn't flee the moment they approached. If possible, they would buy saddles in Melvin Village or a small carriage, but it would take hours to walk to the village.

"Rob, I see a light up ahead," Jo whispered, pulling on the back of his shirt. "On the edge of the woods."

"I see it too," Isobel said quietly, peering through the dark gloom beyond the glow cast by one of the two torches she and Jason carried at the front. "Wait, it's the gypsies."

From the dark depths of the ancient pines, a small wagon approached and drew near before stopping. From the rickety perch, the ancient crone beckoned them closer. "This one has learned her power," she said, staring hard at Jo before a smile creased the skin around her ancient eyes. "You still have more to learn, child, but you no longer fear that which you don't understand. Knowledge comes with time."

"And you, Anasazi," she added, turning to Rob. "You have vanquished the Wendigo. But it is with us still, in soul."

An involuntary shudder rolled over Rob's shoulders. "Surely not, Parvati." He dropped his horse's reins and seized one of the elderly woman's hands. "If not destroyed by fire, then how?"

"It is an undead creature left here long before our time," she said, patting the back of his hand. "It will take years to regenerate itself, but once it does, it will search for you."

"Do not fear, Anasazi," she added as Rob pulled away. Then she chuckled. "You have defeated it once. When you grow stronger... all of you," she added, waving her arm to encompass the entire group, "you will find the way. Now, if you would lift me onto my mule, Anasazi, I will take you into the village in my cart. It is many hours to walk in the dark, and these woods are still not safe."

Deep within the pine forest, a howl sounded in the distance, and they all scampered aboard the dilapidated wagon.

The gypsy woman laughed again. "Don't worry. That's just my grandson. There is far worse than he about in this ancient grove."

CHAPTER TWENTY

They stood as a group around the open grave just outside Melvin Village as Rob lowered the giant skull into the black loam, then drew back. The gypsy woman muttered beneath her breath, then pulled away and climbed into her wagon. "I will leave you now to say the words, Anasazi. I must not hear them, lest they pierce my heart." She drove away in a cloud of dust and disappeared into the forest.

"That one is disturbing, to say the least," Isobel said quite calmly. "I shouldn't care if we never saw her again."

Jo clucked in disgust. "Isobel, stop. If she hadn't helped us, we'd still be walking."

On the eastern horizon, a faint glow peeked red through a dark cloud bank. The morning sun was held back by an approaching storm. In the distance, the village began to awaken, a cock crowing loudly.

"I'm not sure what words to say," Rob said gruffly. "A man of words, I now find myself rather speechless."

Jo clasped his palm with her good hand. In their joined hands, he realized they held an Anasazi arrow. He stared into his wife's beautiful green eyes. In his mind, he heard her soft voice say, "I brought it from the house. I thought we might need it still."

Rob opened his mouth to speak, but odd words spilled forth. "Lord, accept this lost soul and let him finally rest with his people. His work is done, but our day has just begun. We will take up his battle now." The words were uttered in a strange language of which Rob knew nothing, yet somehow Jo understood and nodded in agreement.

From the grave, a swirl of gray dust gathered, growing in size and width until it stretched into the morning light and a vague shape took form: the giant Indian.

He held up one palm in the universal sign of friendship.

"God go with you. I am at peace now," they heard him say. Then a crack of thunder sounded in the distance, and a great roar of wind swept through Melvin Village, kicking up sand in a huge whirlwind. The Anasazi arrow burned red hot in their joined hands, and Rob tried to drop it, but instead, Jo stepped forward and held the arrow up to the disappearing soul before them.

"It is yours now to vanquish evil," the Indian said, then with a whoosh, he was gone.

Jo slumped to the ground, and Rob realized her damaged arm no longer dangled uselessly at her side. Instead, she clasped both hands around the Anasazi arrow, holding it to her chest.

"Jo, you are healed," Rob whispered.

She glanced up, eyes brimming with tears of joy. "He has gone to join his people," she whispered. "At rest finally."

Rob felt such a rush of heat in his chest; unspeakable joy engulfed his body as he drew his wife into his arms. "We are at peace, all of us, at least for the moment," he whispered into her ear as he held her close. "And all because of you."

CHAPTER TWENTY-ONE

The Miriam House in Melvin Village wasn't known for its grandeur or even its food. But the quaint white cottages scattered along the shoreline of Lake Winnipesaukee looked like heaven to Jo.

Rob had settled Isobel and Jason into the cottage next to theirs, throwing a sharp look in Jo's direction, which she read to mean, "Leave it alone. They need to talk."

She doubted talking was at the forefront of her sister's mind, but she had given up on Isobel, who had always possessed a stubborn streak. Over the past week, her sister had shown a fierce determination to strike out on her own.

After spending most of her life sheltering Isobel from the cruel vagaries of the world, it had been difficult to accept the truth over the past week. Jo needed to set Isobel free to make her own way, right or wrong. The time had come for Isobel to spread her wings, to soar, to fail, to fall, and get up again. To find her own strengths—and weaknesses.

"I can't do it for her any longer," she whispered to the wind. "I need to concentrate on Rob and me, our lives together." She let the words swirl away on the foam gathered along the big lake's shoreline.

Rob came up behind her and placed his strong hands on her shoulders. "You can't do what, sweetheart?" She felt the tension slip away as easily as her words.

"I can't pretend anymore," she said, turning to face him. "I've been thinking about us. We need to talk about what we are going to do now, where we will go."

"Why, back to Boston, of course," Rob replied easily, leaning back as he placed his hands around her waist. "And I've been thinking about that honeymoon we never took. Let's go eat lobsters in Maine, or rent a sailboat for the rest of the summer in Lake Placid. Sailing beneath the stars. Doesn't that sound like fun?"

"I don't want to have a honeymoon," Jo said loudly. "I want to have an adventure!"

Rob's eyes held a quizzical look. Was he actually laughing at her? "And this past month hasn't been adventure enough?" he asked drily.

Jo stamped her foot in frustration. "Don't you see? Rob, I've come to understand I can't be afraid my whole life. Otherwise, I'll wake up someday an old woman and realize I never lived my life at all. I don't mean to throw caution to the wind... But to actually live our lives, Rob. Do you understand?"

A wide grin slowly spread over Rob's face. Beneath the grizzled jawline and tired eyes, her husband still looked like the man she had fallen in love with. "*Handsome as the devil,*" she thought as he winked at her.

"Yes, let's go live our lives," he agreed, gathering her hands with his and kissing her knuckles. "After all, this time we might have an 'ordinary' adventure."

She rather doubted that, but the sparkle in Rob's chocolate brown eyes told Jo everything she needed to know.

Her husband had come back to her.

"So, I've been reading about these things out west called Jack-alopes," she remarked. "Perhaps we should go see if we can find some. I mean, how scary can a rabbit be?"

ABOUT THE AUTHOR

Kathleen Greer is a U.S. Army brat, and proud of it. Born in Kyoto, Japan, she spent much of her early childhood living overseas. Particularly, she has fond memories of both Munich and Augsburg, Germany. When her father was not deployed elsewhere, he often read scary fairy tales to Kathy and her older sisters, and she believes this is where she developed a love for the supernatural and horror.

After graduating Summa Cum Laude from New England College in Henniker, New Hampshire, Kathleen headed off with a full scholarship to the University of Pennsylvania Veterinary School. Only to turn it down once she learned she would be required to operate on perfectly healthy beagles who were bred just to be destroyed. She eventually went to work as an investigative reporter at the *Concord Monitor*, a New Hampshire daily, writing under the pen name Kathy Greer. She continued in the newspaper business as a reporter and editor for the *NH Guardian News*, and eventually as the publisher of *UnRavel the Gavel, Inc.* an antiques and collectibles newspaper in New England.

Kathleen now lives in a small, rural town in South Carolina, with her husband Bob, two crazy rescue Boxer pups, Rachel and Joey, a nutty rescue Great Pyrenees mix named Kimba, and about ten rescue cats. "Who can write dark Gothic horror and fantasy without having cats?"

THE END?

Not if you want to dive into more of Crystal Lake Publishing's Tales from the Darkest Depths!

Check out our amazing website and online store or download our latest catalog here.

We always have great new projects and content on the website to dive into, as well as a newsletter, behind the scenes options, social media platforms, our own dark fiction shared-world series and our very own webstore. Our webstore even has categories specifically for KU books, non-fiction, anthologies, and of course more novels and novellas.

Readers...

Thank you for reading *The Wendigo Hunter*. We hope you enjoyed this novella.

If you have a moment, please review *The Wendigo Hunter* at the store where you bought it.

Help other readers by telling them why you enjoyed this book. No need to write an in-depth discussion. Even a single sentence will be greatly appreciated. Reviews go a long way to helping a book sell, and are great for an author's career. It'll also help us to continue publishing quality books.

Thank you again for taking the time to journey with Crystal Lake's Crystal Cove Press.

You will find links to all our social media platforms on our Linktree page: https://linktr.ee/CrystalCovePress.

Follow us on Amazon:

MISSION STATEMENT

Since its founding in August 2012, Crystal Lake has quickly become one of the world's leading publishers of Dark Fiction and Horror books. In 2023, Crystal Lake officially transitioned into an entertainment company, joining several other divisions, genres, and imprints, including Torrid Waters, Sinister Smile Press, Crystal Lake Comics, Crystal Lake Games, Crystal Cove Press, Crystal Lake Kids, Memento Mori Ink, and The House of Shadows & Ink on YouTube.

While we strive to present only the highest quality fiction and entertainment, we also endeavor to support authors along their writing journey. We offer our time and experience in non-fiction projects, as well as author mentoring and services, at competitive prices.

With several Bram Stoker Award wins and many other wins and nominations (including the HWA's Specialty Press Award), Crystal Lake puts integrity, honor, and respect at the forefront of our publishing operations.

We strive for each book and outreach program we spearhead to not only entertain and touch or comment on issues that affect our readers, but also to strengthen and support the Dark Fiction field and its authors.

Not only do we find and publish authors we believe are destined for greatness, but we strive to work with men and women who endeavor to be decent human beings who care more for others than themselves, while still being hard-working, driven, and passionate artists and storytellers.

Crystal Lake is and will always be a beacon of what passion and dedication, combined with overwhelming teamwork and respect, can accomplish. We endeavor to know each and every one of our readers, while building personal relationships with our authors, reviewers, bloggers, podcasters, bookstores, and libraries.

We will be as trustworthy, forthright, and transparent as any business can be, while also keeping most of the headaches away from our authors, since it's our job to solve the problems so they can stay in a creative mind. Which of course also means paying our authors.

We do not just publish books, we present to you worlds within your world, doors within your mind, from talented authors who sacrifice so much for a moment of your time.

There are some amazing small presses out there, and through collaboration and open forums we will continue to support other presses in the goal of helping authors and showing the world what quality small presses are capable of accomplishing. No one wins when a small press goes down, so we will always be there to support hardworking, legitimate presses and their authors. We don't see Crystal Lake as the best press out there, but we will always strive to be the best, strive to be the most interactive and grateful, and even blessed press around. No matter what happens over time, we will also take our mission very seriously while appreciating where we are and enjoying the journey.

What do we offer our authors that they can't do for themselves through self-publishing?

We are big supporters of self-publishing (especially hybrid publishing), if done with care, patience, and planning. However, not every author has the time or inclination to do market research, advertise, and set up book launch strategies. Although a lot of authors are successful in doing it all, strong small presses will always be there for the authors who just want to do what they do best: write.

What we offer is experience, industry knowledge, contacts and trust built up over years. And due to our strong brand and trusting fanbase, every Crystal Lake book comes with weight of respect. In time our fans begin to trust our judgment and will try a new author purely based on our support of said author.

To date we've published around 300 books, and with each launch we strive to fine-tune our approach, learn from our mistakes, and increase our reach. We continue to assure our authors that we're here for them and that we'll carry the weight of the launch and deal with third parties while they focus on their strengths—be it writing, interviews, blogs, signings, etc.

We also offer several mentoring packages to authors that include knowledge and skills they can use in both traditional and self-publishing endeavors. This includes Shadows & Ink Creators on our The House of Shadows & Ink YouTube channel and our Crystal Lake Academy.

We look forward to launching many new careers. This is what we believe in. What we stand for. This will be our legacy.

**Welcome to Crystal Lake Publishing—
Where Stories Come Alive!**